PROMISES TO KEEP

Also by Susan Wojciechowski:

And the Other, Gold
Patty Dillman of Hot Dog Fame

SUSAN WOJCIECHOWSKI

PROMISES TO KEEP

CROWN PUBLISHERS, INC.
New York

Published by Crown Publishers, Inc., a Random House company, 225 Park Avenue South,
New York, New York 10003

CROWN is a trademark of Crown Publishers, Inc.
Manufactured in the United States of America
Library of Congress Cataloging-in-Publication Data
Wojciechowski, Susan.
Promises to keep / Susan Wojciechowski.
p. cm.
Summary: Eighth-grader Patty Dillman makes a New Year's resolution
to become friends with the popular and rich Penni Pendleton.
[1. Friendship—Fiction. 2. Interpersonal relations—Fiction.]
I. Title.
PZ7.W818568Pr 1991
[Fic]—dc20   90-23437
ISBN 0-517-58186-8 (trade)
0-517-58187-6 (lib. bdg.)
10 9 8 7 6 5 4 3 2 1
First Edition

To Carol—
my sister, my friend

ACKNOWLEDGMENTS

Thank you to Fred Nichols for candidly sharing his past, and offering a glimpse into prison life

Thank you to Cephas-Attica for helping Fred to come back, and give back, and keep some promises

Thank you to the young Rochester, New York, poets whose work appears on these pages: Deanna Fleysher ("Sun Cat"), Amy Knorr ("While Camping with Friends"), Scott Lowe ("Standing Alone"), Michael Mounts (untitled), Brian Mulford ("The Hole"), and Jennifer Serio ("Things I Fear")

1

It was the last night of Christmas vacation and Tracy and I were trying our best to ignore the fact. I was propped against my headboard biting my nails and Tracy, who's been my best friend since we were three, was lying next to me twirling her long, blond braid and half-heartedly humming along with a Bruce Springsteen tape. Tracy had just gotten back from a ski trip sponsored by the rec center, so we had some catching up to do, but our hearts weren't in it.

"Over vacation I played twenty-six games of Hungry, Hungry Hippos with my little sister, and the three times I didn't let her win, she threw all the marbles across the room and kicked me," I reported to Tracy.

"At the ski resort I puked the first time I rode up the chair lift," Tracy told me.

"I got a zit on my chin yesterday," I offered.

PROMISES TO KEEP

"I took a pound of red licorice twists on the trip and ate them all the first night," Tracy informed me.

"No wonder you puked on the lift."

"I prefer to blame it on the broccoli casserole they served at the lodge," Tracy said.

"I learned to play chess last week," I mentioned.

"I got frostbite on my earlobes my last day on the slopes," she told me as she rolled over onto her stomach and sighed.

"We're pathetic," I said after a few minutes.

"You got that right," Tracy answered, and sighed again.

The grandfather clock in the downstairs hall chimed eleven times, which meant it was eight o'clock. It's been chiming three hours ahead of itself ever since my weenie brother Chris, who's eight, was learning to tell time and practiced by moving the hands to different positions.

"Hey," Tracy said, jumping off the bed so hard my head bounced on the headboard. "It's getting late. Let's not end the vacation talking about complexion problems and barfing. What do you say we go over to Gary's house and bug him? I swore I'd get even with him when he wedged himself between me and Scott Wandover the whole five-hour bus ride home from the ski trip. We could set his hair on fire or something."

Gary Holmes has lived four houses from me for as long as I can remember. He's in eighth grade at Saint Ignatius Junior High, like Tracy and me, and has had a crush on me ever since he's had hormones. He kissed me once, when he brought me home from the seventh-grade dance, but luckily I was wearing spike heels at the time. I rammed my heel down on his foot so hard he still walks with a slight limp. It's not that he's ugly or anything, he's just Gary, someone who's always there but you don't notice, sort of like wallpaper.

2

Tracy grabbed our jackets and threw mine at me while she called to my parents that we were going over to Gary's house to tuck him in. I didn't even get a chance to comb my hair. Not that I cared. It was only Gary we were going to see, not a real guy or anything.

"I hope he's home alone," Tracy said as we rang the doorbell.

"I bet he is. Monday is his parents' bowling league night and his brother went back to college yesterday."

Gary answered the door wearing red plaid pajamas and slippers that looked like tigers' paws. His light blond hair was hanging in his eyes, as usual, and he jerked his head back to flip the hair out of his way, as usual. He jerks his head so much that when you're with him for a while, you start doing it too.

"Hi, dollface," he said to me.

"Hi, trollface," Tracy answered for both of us.

"Care to come in, Patty?" Gary said, putting his arm around my shoulder. "You'll have to leave your pet outside, though." Tracy reached over and flicked his arm away from me. She pushed her way past him and into the living room.

"So, what can I do for you?" Gary asked.

"Well," I stammered. "Umm. Computer paper. That's it. I'd like to borrow some."

"I've got plenty and the price is right—a kiss for every sheet. This could take all night, dollface," he said, jerking his head back.

"You're brain-damaged," Tracy said. "Did your mother drop you on your head when you were a baby? Out a third-story window?"

"Yeah, and I landed on you."

"It's okay," I cut in. "The paper's for my father. I'll send him right over to pay and I'll be sure to tell him to put on Chap Stick before he comes."

"Gotcha!" Tracy laughed to Gary as he left to get the paper. As soon as he was gone she asked me to stall him for a few minutes.

"Those tiger slippers gave me an idea," she said. "We're going to borrow his entire wardrobe of footwear, except for those slippers. Tomorrow morning he'll go hyper when he realizes he has nothing to wear to school but his Tony the Tiger feet. Then we'll call him up at the last minute and tell him where his shoes are." Tracy disappeared into the kitchen. A couple of minutes later she snuck up the stairs, dragging a huge plastic garbage bag behind her.

When Gary came back with the paper he didn't even notice Tracy had left. He sat next to me on the couch and tried to be smooth.

"Now, what else can I do for you, dollface?" he asked, jerking his head back.

"For starters you can back off, kitty litter breath."

Gary sighed and moved to the other end of the couch. He flipped his legs up and landed his tiger feet in my lap. Gary is very muscular from being on the wrestling team, and his legs weighed a ton, but I resisted the urge to dump them off me.

He told me he was sorry that I couldn't scrape up the money to go on the Christmas ski trip, because I missed watching his smooth style, on the slopes and off. Then he proceeded to name all the girls who had thrown themselves at him the whole five days of the trip.

"Very interesting, Gary. I love fairy tales," I said. I kept yawning big, exaggerated yawns while he bragged.

4

"Speaking of fairy tales, I hear your prince charming broke up with you," Gary said.

I stiffened when I heard the words. I knew Gary was referring to Tim Shokow, who used to be my boyfriend till we broke up right before Christmas, mainly because Tim liked skiing a lot more than he liked being with me. Tim is on the football team at St. Iggie's. He has light brown, almost blond hair that's short in front but sort of curls up longer at the back of his neck. When he smiles he has a dimple by his mouth that makes my knees go weak. He's muscular and what you'd call a hunk. I still have hopes of getting him back.

"Where did you hear that?" I asked, trying to sound nonchalant.

"Good news travels fast. I also heard he was at Penni Pendleton's New Year's Eve party."

"You think I didn't know that?" I squirmed in my seat. I *hadn't* known that. Suddenly the room felt warm and my scalp started to prickle. I wished Tracy would hurry up.

Just then, out of the corner of my eye I saw Tracy lugging the garbage bag out the front door, so I whapped Gary's legs onto the floor, told him to put a sock in it, and made a quick exit.

"Look," Tracy whispered when I had shut the door behind me. She opened the bag. "It's Gary's entire footwear wardrobe. I even took his wrestling shoes. He won't have a thing to wear to school tomorrow except his geeky tiger slippers."

"This is totally awesome," I said, grinning and jerking my head back. "Tomorrow we can call him, two minutes before the bus comes."

We put the bag on the Holmeses' back porch and ran to my

house. Once we were safely in my room with the door shut we collapsed laughing.

"Tracy," I said, "you are mean and cruel and heartless."

"That's the nicest thing anyone's ever said to me. I think I'm going to cry." Tracy dabbed at her eyes with the corner of my bedspread.

I flopped onto the bed, but Tracy pulled me back up. "We are not going to spend the rest of the night wimping out on the bed," she ordered. "It's your turn to think of something to do."

"Well, let's see," I said. I jerked my head back. "I know. Let's write some New Year's resolutions." I got a stack of filler paper from my desk and we sat on the floor, thinking.

When we were finished Tracy read her list first:

"One—I resolve to clean my room at least twice a year.

"Two—I resolve never to eat a pound of red licorice at one sitting."

"That's it?" I asked. "Aren't you going to try to improve yourself or stop any bad habits or be nicer to your family or anything meaningful?"

"No, I'm pretty much perfect in those areas."

"You are not."

"Am too."

"Are not."

"Am too."

"How about the way you chew on the end of your braid? Isn't that something you could resolve to stop doing?"

"Why? That's how I get my protein."

"Oh, never mind. Listen to my list." I read:

"I, Patricia Dillman, being of sound mind and body"—at this point Tracy giggled and I had to stop and give her a dirty look

6

before reading on—"hereby resolve and promise to achieve the following goals in the coming twelve months:

"One—stop biting my nails.

"Two—be kind and loving to my brothers and sister, unless they do something mean first and I am forced to get even.

"Three—write to my new pen pal in prison at least once a week.

"Four—start reading my fifteen-volume set of the World's Greatest Classics, which my parents gave me on my tenth birthday and which I really, really have been meaning to start.

"Five—let my hair grow long like Penni Pendleton's.

"Six—straighten my hair so it sort of swings from side to side like Penni Pendleton's.

"Seven—wash my face three times a day with cleansing granules so my skin will glow like Penni's.

"Eight—wear cashmere, instead of polyester or acrylic sweaters, like P.P.

"Nine—sit near P.P.'s lunch table to hear how she talks and what she talks about.

"Ten—change the spelling of my name to P-a-t-t-i.

"Eleven—get invited to parties at P.P.'s.

"Twelve—get boys to drool over me.

"Thirteen—get diamond earrings like P.P.'s."

Tracy looked at me like I was totally nutso and asked me what the heck was going on with me all of a sudden.

"I just decided that I want to change my image, that's all. I want to be totally cool like Penni."

"When did all this happen? In the last six seconds?"

"I've just been thinking that I want to be more refined, that's all. And Penelope Pendleton is a model of refinement and class."

PROMISES TO KEEP

It's weird how Penni totally stands out at St. Iggie's. We all wear the same uniform as a symbol of equality and to discourage emphasis on materialism. But Penni, wearing the standard-issue plaid skirt, navy vest, and regulation shoes that look like combat boots, always manages to look better than everyone else, with her diamond earrings, tortoiseshell barrettes, designer purses, and the cashmere sweater she drapes over her shoulders the minute there's the slightest breeze. Of course, it helps that she's also gorgeous.

"Well, I hardly know Penni," Tracy said. "I mean, she just came to St. Iggie's last September. But she seems kind of phony to me."

"Yeah, well, those diamond earrings she wears sure aren't phony, and the Jaguar she gets driven to school in sure isn't phony, and the way all the guys drool over her is real."

Tracy lay down on the floor and started doing sit-ups. "Look," she said, trying to talk and count sit-ups at the same time, "just be satisfied, eleven, with who you are, twelve. You may not be, thirteen, Miss Popularity, fourteen, but you've had a few guys, fifteen, drool over you in your career, sixteen."

"Name three."

Tracy stopped doing sit-ups so she could count off the names on her fingers. "There's Tim Shokow. There's Gary Holmes, and . . . and . . . there's that boy who used to sit behind you in third grade, I can't remember his name."

"His name was George Lunk and he didn't drool over me, he just plain drooled on account of his overbite," I said. "As for Gary Holmes, he doesn't count. And Tim drooled only when he had nothing better to do, like when he wasn't drooling over a football or a ski slope. Oh, Trace, I just want to know what it feels like

8

to be invited to cool parties and be part of the popular crowd that kids like Penni belong to. I want to change my image. I'm tired of being a big fat zero. I want to be special, I want to stand out, like Penni. I heard she has an indoor pool and over Thanksgiving break she had a beach party. Everyone who came had to dress in tropical clothes. Then, guess what? She gave out huge beach towels as favors. Can you believe it? At my last birthday party I gave out stupid bookmarks as favors."

"Hey, I love my Garfield bookmark. I use it all the time," Tracy cut in.

"You would."

"What do you mean by that crack?"

"I mean, you and I are the same—dull and ordinary. And I'm going to change. I'm going to be cool and sophisticated like Penni. How about you?"

Tracy looked at me. "I don't know, Pats. I could be wrong, but I get the feeling Penni thinks she's better than anybody else 'cause she's rich. I've heard some kids at school call her 'Princess Penni.' I'd rather steer clear of her."

"Maybe she really *is* better than anybody else. I mean, she's lived in Europe and gets driven to school by a chauffeur and has her initials monogrammed on just about every piece of clothing she owns. Joanne Zawacki's in gym with Penni and she said Penni wears monogrammed silk underwear."

"Oh, I didn't realize monogrammed underwear makes you better than anybody else," Tracy said sarcastically. "Look, if monogrammed Fruit of the Looms turn you on, that's one thing, but don't try to be like Penni just so people will notice you."

"Actually, I don't want just anyone to notice me. I want to be sophisticated and cool so Tim will notice me. I heard he got invited to Penni's New Year's Eve party."

"Scott Wandover got invited too. They got invited because they're on the football team."

"But Tim went. Maybe he likes her type. Maybe if I'm more like her or get to be friends with her he'll like me again."

"Give it up, Pats, will you? You and Tim are old news. Hasn't it sunk in yet? I mean, you even took ski lessons to try to hold on to Tim and it didn't work. You're just not right for each other. Don't be something you're not just to get him back."

"We are too right for each other."

"Are not."

"Are too."

"Are not."

"Well, whether we are or not, would you just humor me along by helping me keep my resolutions?"

"How? By giving you my allowance every week so you can buy a new wardrobe? No way."

"No, just poke me when I bite my nails and remind me to be nice to my sleazoid brother Chris, and just generally check up on me to make sure I stick with my resolutions."

"Okay, I'll do it, but only because if I say no you'll pester me day and night till I change my mind. You're a mega pest and I don't know why I've let you be my best friend for the past ten years. I guess I just feel sorry for you. You're such a pathetic creature."

I punched Tracy on the arm, then hugged her.

"Look, I've got to go home now," she said, checking her watch. "Walk me halfway?"

So we walked across the Easton College campus, where I live in faculty housing since my father's head of the English department. I left Tracy at the main road and went back home, trying to picture myself at a famous Penni Pendleton party. I pictured Tim there, looking up and seeing me walk in wearing huge diamond earrings, a white leather skirt, and a hand-knit sweater imported from someplace other than Taiwan. I pictured our eyes locking and him leaving Penni standing alone by a huge marble fireplace to come over to me and lead me out onto the balcony. We'd look up at the black, starry night. His arm would go around me and he'd ask me to take him back. I'd laugh a tinkling, light laugh. My hair would swing softly against my shoulders. Tim would brush a stray strand from my cheek and then take my face in his hands and gently . . .

"Hey, bonehead, watch out! You're about to walk into a tree." It was my twelve-year-old brother, Joel, in the driveway shoveling snow. He shook his head and mumbled something under his breath as I walked past him.

Before I got into bed I took my diary from behind the gold-lettered set of the World's Greatest Classics on my bookshelf and stuck my list of resolutions into it. Then I polished my nails as a reminder not to bite them, brushed my hair a hundred strokes to help it grow, scrubbed my face with cleansing granules, and went to sleep.

2

At breakfast the next morning I let out a giggle every time I pictured Gary racing around in his ridiculous slippers looking for his shoes.

"Now that's what I like to see," said my dad, "a young lady who's happy and eager to get back to school." Then he looked at Joel and Chris and said, "Why don't you two try to follow your sister's example?"

"Because my sister wouldn't be smiling on the day we go back to school," Joel grumbled as he glared at me. "An alien has obviously taken possession of Patty's body. Quick—if you're my sister answer this: What year and in what subject did you change a final grade on your report card?"

Dad's eyebrows shot up and he looked at me for an answer.

"He's joking, Dad. You know I would never do anything like that."

"Okay, that proves it," Joel said, grabbing my shoulders. "You *are* from another galaxy. Come on now, out with it. What have you done with my sister?"

Just then Tracy came in the side door, took a buttered bagel from the table, and sat down with us. She looked at me and we both cracked up.

"Another alien. They're taking over the planet," Joel said. He grabbed his books and left.

"We'd better get moving too," I warned Tracy. "It's zero hour minus three minutes." We took the telephone into the hall closet and I dialed Gary's number. His mother answered and told me he couldn't come to the phone because he was running late.

"Tell him it's urgent," I said, trying to stifle a laugh. When Gary came on the phone I told him to go look on the back porch and he'd find a big surprise. I hung up and Tracy and I ran for the bus.

"Patty, phone," my mother called out the front door as we reached the sidewalk. "Gary Holmes. He says it's urgent."

Gary sounded impatient. "Is this surprise on your back porch or mine?" he asked.

"Yours. You mean you didn't find it?"

"Not unless the surprise is a pot of dead geraniums, a broken toboggan, or a folding lawn chair with a foot of snow on it."

I dropped the phone and ran for his yard. Gary was waiting there, his feet wedged into his mother's pink bowling shoes. We looked on the front porch and the back porch and in all the bushes. The plastic trash bag had disappeared. The school bus had also come and gone by the time we gave up looking.

My mom drove all of us to school. She wasn't too happy about it, especially since we were all kind of vague about why we missed the bus. In the car, no one said a word, except for my

three-year-old sister, Mary, who spent the entire ride begging
Mom to buy her some pink shoes like Gary's.

"I think Gary's bluffing," Tracy announced at lunch as she
unwrapped her bologna and ketchup sandwich. The gang
agreed—the gang being Allison Stenclik, who was on the hockey
team with Tracy last year; Trish Hoffman, who I met last fall
when we were in a school play together; Kate Donnelly, my
second-best friend since elementary school; Jeannie Croydon, a
superbrain I got to know because we work on the school paper
together; and Whitney Wixsome, who Kate went up to one day
in fifth grade and told her that she loved the sound of her name.
They've been friends ever since. By the way, Whitney is gorgeous.

"I don't think he's bluffing," I said. "No sane person would
wear bowling shoes, especially pink bowling shoes that are three
sizes too small, for a full day just to get even. No, Tracy. Someone
took that trash bag and we're responsible."

"The key word here is 'sane,' " Tracy answered. "You know
and I know and the entire planet knows that Gary is as nutty
as a jar of Planters peanuts. So let's just stay calm and call his
bluff. If he doesn't show up tomorrow in his ugly brown St.
Iggie's regulation oxfords I'll stand on my head on the front
lawn of school and play 'The Star-Spangled Banner' on my
trumpet."

We avoided Gary for the rest of the day. Of course, at St.
Iggie's that's not hard to do. Our school is coinstitutional, which
means that males and females go there, but they don't have
classes together. The building is split into two sections. The boys
have their classes on one side and the girls have theirs on the

other. The only things we share are the cafeteria, library, and gym. As you can probably guess, we all spend a lot of time doing research in the library.

The following morning I was nervous as I stood at the bus stop. Tracy didn't look too sure of herself either. She kept twirling her braid and glancing in the direction of Gary's house. Finally we saw him coming toward us. He seemed to be walking funny. As he got closer I realized it was because he was wearing his mother's bowling shoes again. The bus pulled up. Tracy and I leaped onto it and tried to hide in back row seats. Gary came down the aisle and sat right in front of us, sticking his feet out to the side. He didn't speak to us the whole ride. But as he got off the bus at school he turned around and said, "My house. Four P.M. Be there."

"Got your trumpet handy?" I growled to Tracy as we split up to go to our lockers.

Tracy came to my house after school. We ran up to my room and I handed her a sheet of filler paper.

"Okay, what was in the bag? Make a list and figure out how much we owe Gary."

What Tracy could remember was: ratty brown school shoes, white Nike leather sneakers (laces missing), black wrestling shoes, red cloth high-top sneakers (gross-smelling), brown suede hiking boots, penny loafers, blue terry-cloth slippers (hole in toe).

I looked at the list. "I bet he even makes us pay back the pennies for the penny loafers. Trace, this is going to cost a fortune. I don't have a cent."

"Got any bonds you could cash in? Or could you borrow some money from Joel? He's always loaded."

"He's always cheap, too. How much do you have?"

"I spent everything on the ski trip. I'm flat busted," Tracy said, shaking her head. "Do you realize the blackmail he's capable of? I could be forced to do his homework for a year. You could be forced to go steady with him."

"I'd rather be thrown naked into a pond of bloodsucking leeches."

"Don't give him any ideas."

We sighed and put on our jackets. We rang Gary's doorbell. His mother led us into the living room and called Gary down.

"It'll take him a while," she said. "The poor boy can barely walk. I can't believe what they make the kids do for initiation into clubs these days. If Gary ends up with bunions from being forced to wear those pink bowling shoes for two days, I'll sue the school, I swear." Just then Gary came in.

"And I hope you moved that trash bag full of shoes from the middle of your bedroom floor, young man," his mom said as she turned to leave the room. "I nearly tripped over it vacuuming today."

Gary looked wildly toward the stairs, gauging if he could outrun us. Before he could make a move Tracy and I jumped on top of him right in front of his mother. While I pummeled his back Tracy stuffed our list into his mouth. Then we each yanked off one of his bowling shoes and started hitting him.

"You sleazoid!" I yelled as I whapped him. "You had that bag all along!"

"I'll be glad when this initiation business is over with," his mother mumbled, shaking her head.

By the time we got back to my house Tracy and I were laughing so hard tears were running down our cheeks. We went up to my room and flopped on the bed.

"Can you believe," I said, "he wore those ridiculous bowling shoes for two solid days just to get even with us?"

"Yeah, and he had to go to the principal's office to explain not being in uniform. I wonder what he used as an excuse."

"Better yet, what excuse did he give the other guys for wearing pink shoes?"

"I loved the look on his face when his mother said to move the trash bag."

While we were laughing Chris poked his head in the door. "What's the joke?"

"Your face," I told him. "And knock before you barge in."

Chris slammed the door and went clattering down the stairs. "Mommmm! Patty's making fun of me, and she's sitting on her new bedspread with her shoes on."

"You want a little brother?" I asked Tracy. "I'll pay you to take him."

"You don't have any money, remember?"

"Oh, yeah. Well, at least we didn't end up having to figure out a way to pay Gary for his shoes."

"And we had a good laugh," Tracy added. "That Gary's a cool dude."

"You're kidding."

She wasn't kidding.

3

That night, just after the grandfather clock chimed twelve times (translation: nine o'clock), Tracy called.

"This isn't a social call, it's a business call," she said. "It's my duty to inform you that you already broke two of your resolutions."

"Did not."

"Did too."

"Did not."

"Did too."

"Which ones?"

"Number one, you bit your nails while we were waiting for Gary at his house."

"That doesn't count. I was majorly spazzing out and it was either bite my nails or start puking. What's the other resolution I broke?"

"You were creepy to your brother when he came into your room this afternoon."

"That doesn't count either. He did something mean first by barging in. On all the other resolutions I'm doing just fine," I told her as I took the phone into the hall closet for privacy.

"You don't sound like you mean it," Tracy said. "Get out the list and let's go through it one by one."

So I went upstairs and pulled the list out of my journal.

"Number one—biting nails—and number two—being nice— I explained. Number three—writing to prison pen pal. I just got his first letter today and I'll answer it tomorrow. I'll read you his letter after you finish interrogating me. Number four—reading the World's Greatest Classics. I was just about to start them when you called. All the rest of the stuff about changing my image I'm going to start tomorrow. And the resolution about boys drooling over me—well, I've got three hundred sixty-two more days to make that one happen. Satisfied?"

"Well, I'm a little disappointed. Try to do better tomorrow."

"What are you, my mother? Are you going to give me the third degree every ten minutes?"

"You're the one who practically begged me to, and now you're getting touchy. I wouldn't act that way if you pointed out that I broke any of my resolutions," Tracy said self-righteously.

"Yeah, right. Like you're in supreme danger of shoveling a pound of red licorice into your face every day."

"Does this mean you don't want me to help you keep your resolutions?"

"Not if the only thing you do is watch every move I make and gloat every time I slip up."

"Okay, let's compromise. I'll just keep track of your nail biting. Deal?"

"Deal. Now let me read you my pen pal letter."

The reason I received a letter from a prisoner is that we have a pen pal program at our school between students and prison inmates. It was started by Sister Clarabelle, one of the teachers at St. Iggie's. Her name is actually Sister Barbara Clare, but she has this big red nose, so we all call her Sister Clarabelle the Clown.

Anyway, Sister Clarabelle decided that it would be good for the inmates at Smithville Penitentiary to get to know regular kids and for us kids to find out what lands people in the slammer.

"And basically," Sister Clarabelle said, "you children will find out how very much alike we all are." Give me a break! No way am I like my pen pal, who's in jail for armed robbery of some banks.

The way I got to be a pen pal is that I'm in Sister Clarabelle's religion class and she said all those who volunteer to be pen pals get extra credit on their religion grade. So of course, I volunteered. I need all the help I can get.

I opened the closet door to get some light and settled back against the vacuum cleaner to read the letter.

Dear Patty,

First thing is thanks for writing to me. Nobody writes to me but my ma and my sister and every day when the guard comes with the mail I lay on my bed and hope he'll stick a letter through my bars. I hardly ever get none. I hope you keep writing to me.

Second thing is they told you my name is William but nobody calls me that. Its my born name but everybody calls me Fango. How I got that name was on acount of I always liked to draw even when I was a kid so my big brother one time asked me Who do you think you are—Van Gogh? So my baby brother hear him call me Van Gogh only the baby said it wrong and it came out Fango. So hes all the time calling me Fango and pretty soon nobody remembers my real name.

I got to tell you something grate just happened to me about drawing. A picture I drew got put in an art show at a college near here and it won the Peoples Choice Award. That means everyone who came voted for there favorite picture and mine got the most votes. So I get called in the wardens office and he gave me a trophy as big as your arm and some guy there takes pictures for the Smithville newspaper and everybody shakes my hand and smiles. Then everybody leaves and I just start to look at the trophy and the warden takes it away from me cause I could turn it into a wepon. He tells me he dont make the rules he just enforce them. So I tell him send the trophy to my ma and tell her to put it on the tv and dont sell it unless she realy needs the money.

You sure asked a ton of questions in your letter and I will answer them all. It sounds like you want to know every last thing about this place. Well, I will tell you one thing right off. This aint no country club.

First thing is that Im in prison for armed robbery of banks. I got 3½ to 7 years. I been inside for almost 4 years but it seems like 40.

You want to know what it looks like in prison so Ill tell you. My cell is so narrow I can reach the sides if I put my arms out and its about 12 feet long. I got a bed with a thin matress and a sink with just cold water and a toilet. I got a cubbord on the floor two feet high to keep all my stuff. The walls and floor are gray and you best believe me when I tell you its dull. You could get depresed in here even if the door wasnt locked. I got to tell *you a funny thing happened. One day I was sleeping and my head rolled sideways off the edge of the bed and it landed in the toilet. What a way to wake yourself up. I didnt need no snooz alarm that day Ha-ha.*

Your not suposed to put things on the walls. They probly think your drilling a hole behind them to escape. But I tape stuff to my walls anyway. About once a month they make you take the things down. But then I just put them back up.

You asked me to go back to day number one and tell you my story because of you wanting to be a writer so I will do that in my next letter cause my hand is geting tired right now. But just remember one thing—when you write my story I get half the money you make off it. Just kidding—ha-ha.

Please write back.

Can I ask you a riddle? I will answer it in my next letter if you dont get it right. Riddle—what makes more noise when it is dead than when it is alive?

from
Fango

PS I hope you write back.

"That's awesome," Tracy said when I had finished the letter. "What kinds of questions did you ask him?"

"Oh, stuff like how he got to be in trouble with the law and what it's like to get arrested and what he does all day, stuff like that. It really feels creepy to be writing to a real live convict."

Before Tracy hung up she dictated a list of questions she wanted Fango to answer.

I hung up the phone and took the letter upstairs to tuck it in the bottom drawer of my desk, where I keep all my small important stuff. The bottom desk drawer holds snapshots, 3-D glasses, receipts, movie stubs, bubble gum cartoons, greeting cards, birthday party invitations, and a deflated balloon that this guy gave me last year when a bunch of us girls were at Geneva Lake Amusement Park. Some guys started following us around, and when we rode the merry-go-round one of them stood next to the horse I was on and put his arm around my waist. Then he bought me a helium balloon and took my phone number, but he never called me.

In the drawer are also piles of letters. I've got letters from my cousin Nancy, letters from home when I've been at camp, letters from sweepstakes telling me I may have already won a million dollars, notes passed to me in class from Tracy—at least the ones that weren't confiscated by teachers—and notes from Tim Shokow.

My big important stuff is under the bed: like old dolls, stuffed animals, yearbooks, school newspapers, awards, crafts from as far back as kindergarten, the model of the solar system I made in fourth grade—things like that.

My mom says I could open up a souvenir shop with all the stuff I've collected over the years. But I can't help it if I'm sentimental. I tell her that someday when I'm a famous journalist it'll all be worth money.

I read my list of resolutions over once more and decided that tomorrow I would start "Project Cool." I would become like Penelope Pendleton and find out what it feels like to be one of the popular group. I would laugh her tinkling laugh, not my nasal snort that Joel says sounds like a pig who's just heard a dirty joke. I would talk in her slow, throaty voice that causes everyone to turn and pay attention, instead of squawking, "Hey, you guys, listen up!" whenever I want to get the gang's attention. I would get her to invite me to her parties, where Tim Shokow would notice me and wonder why he ever decided to dump me.

I climbed into bed with a volume of my gold-lettered, imitation-leather-bound set of the World's Greatest Classics. The book was *Oliver Twist,* and the very first sentence was eight lines long, full of commas and colons and hyphens. I fell asleep trying to figure out what the heck Charles Dickens was trying to say.

4

"Mom, can I borrow your diamond chip earrings to wear to school?" I yelled down the stairs the next morning.

"Not unless you're being presented with a Nobel Prize today at assembly," she yelled back.

"Yes, I am."

"On second thought, I'd like to be there. I think I'll wear them."

"Har-har. Thanks a lot, Mom. Remind me never to lend you any of my stuff."

I came downstairs wearing my usual tiny gold-plated loop earrings.

"Dad, can I have diamond earrings for Valentine's Day?"

"Sure. Just tell the big spender who's buying them to be sure and get them insured."

I sat down at the table and ran my fingers through my hair

to push it away from my face, the way I'd seen Penni do it. But in my case, my fingers were running mostly through the air because my hair is so darned short. It's not only short but naturally curly, too. I hate it. No matter how much I mousse it and spray it, my hair pops out in any direction it feels like.

While I'm on the subject let me say that I'm not particularly crazy about the rest of me, either. I'm so totally ordinary. I have these ordinary green eyes which would look good if they could just be highlighted with a little green eye shadow, but my mom won't let me wear any. And my nose is totally ordinary, except that it's sort of rounded at the end, which I hate. A little liquid makeup in a shade darker than my skin, blended along the sides of my nose, would fix that. It said so in 'Teen magazine. But my mom won't let me use liquid makeup, either. She treats me like such a child. My mouth is ordinary too. It's sort of full and I hope someday that will look sexy, but for now it doesn't. I inherited a square face from my father's side of the family and my dad says it makes me look like I have strong character, whatever that means.

My body isn't even worth mentioning, take my word for it. Joel says if I turn sideways you can't see me. I inherited the skinny body from my mother's side of the family. My mother's figure is not much better than mine, and she's thirty-eight years old. So I'm not going to hold my breath waiting to fill out. Honestly, I can't believe my mother breast-fed us four kids with what little equipment she has. But she says she nursed each of us till we started to bite, and it was the most satisfying experience of her life (the nursing, not the biting), next to childbirth, which was absolute heaven, to hear her talk about it.

One time I set her straight on that score. I told her we had seen a movie on childbirth in health class and every single girl in the room decided not to have kids, it was so gross. But she only smiled and said, "You just wait."

As I practiced running my fingers through my hair Chris asked, "What are you trying to do, shake the cooties off your head?" I ignored the comment and asked him, in my Penni Pendleton voice, to please pass the milk.

"You got a frog in your throat?" he wanted to know.

"No, my sweet little silly." I laughed softly. "I'm just trying to cultivate a genteel demeanor."

Chris shoved the milk carton down the table and moved his chair farther away from me. "Mom, Patty's talking weird," he whined as he snarfed down his cereal, drooling milk all over his chin.

"Can't you be a little more refined?" I asked him. "Try not to act like your food's in a trough. Mom, I think Chris missed school the day they taught table manners."

"Yeah, and Chris passed everything he knows down to Mary," Joel said with a laugh. Mary was sitting in her high chair, banging on the tray with her little spoon with the ceramic bunny on the handle, yelling, "Me want Cocoa Butts. Me want Honey Mutts." Mom doesn't allow us to have sweet cereal, but Mary has demanded it every day for the past three months. Joel and I have a bet going. I say that before the end of January Mom will jump up from the table some morning and go running wild-eyed to the supermarket for sweet cereal just to shut the kid up. Joel bets Mom'll hold on to her principles.

That morning Mom sat clutching the edge of the table all through breakfast. The end was near. I figured it was a matter of days before five dollars would come floating into my wallet.

PROMISES TO KEEP

At lunch I suggested to the gang that we find a different table to sit at, just for a change of view. Then I steered us to a table right next to Penelope Pendleton's. I picked a seat that was back to back with Penni's and leaned my chair back a little so I could hear what she said and how she talked.

I was just getting settled when Tracy interrupted my eavesdropping to check on whether I'd remembered to bring Fango's letter from home to read to the gang. After I read it she asked everybody to tell me any questions they might have for him. Trish wanted me to find out if they at least have little curtains or something in front of the toilets in their cells. She couldn't believe they have to go to the bathroom right out in the open where anyone walking by can see.

"Who'd be walking by?" Tracy asked. "It's prison. Everybody's locked up."

By the time I had listed everybody's questions lunch was nearly over and I spotted Gary Holmes heading our way. He squeezed past Tracy and Kate to get to me.

"Hey, dollface," Gary blared, so loud that Penni turned around and said, "Ugh, I hope whatever he has isn't catching."

I tried to pretend he wasn't talking to me. I didn't want Penni to think I knew someone with something catching.

"Hey, dollface Dillman," Gary said, louder this time. "I've got a proposition for you. Can we talk?"

"No, we cannot talk. Can't you see I'm busy?" I whispered.

I heard Penni say to her friends, "St. Iggie's must be hard up. They take anything that walks on two legs." Everyone at her table laughed.

"I need to talk to you and I've got all the time in the world to wait," Gary said, smiling. He jerked his head back to get the hair out of his eyes and stood there embarrassing the heck out of me.

28

"See me after school, at my house. I'll set aside four o'clock till four-oh-two," I hissed. "Now will you please disintegrate?"

Gary left and I leaned my chair back again, hoping to get in at least a few minutes of eavesdropping. Penni laughed a lot and it seemed like everyone at her table hung on every word she said. She talked mostly about horseback riding lessons and I was starting to get bored till I heard the word "party" mentioned.

Of course, Trish chose that moment to complain at about a hundred decibels, "Why the hey are we so far from the ice cream counter?"

"Stifle it," I said, waving my hand at Trish and leaning farther back to hear about the party. Just then the rear legs of my chair slid out from under me. My chair fell backward right against Penni. She got wedged against her table and had the wind knocked out of her.

Then I felt my chair going down. I felt my body sliding under the table. I heard everyone gasp. Finally I heard Penni shove herself back and growl at me, "Clumsy!" She stood up and walked away, her entourage following her, after they all glared at me.

"Go breathe exhaust fumes," Tracy called after them as she reached under the table and pulled me out.

"Quiet!" I warned her. "I had it coming. I could have hurt Penni."

I spent the last few minutes of lunch with my head down, scratching circles in my waxed paper and wishing I could evaporate into thin air.

I decided that from then on I'd sit across the table, where I could watch Penni at a safe distance.

PROMISES TO KEEP

At four o'clock that afternoon I was standing, paintbrush in hand, at the blackboard that hangs in the side entry of our old Victorian house. The blackboard is divided into six columns, one for each member of the family, and is for writing messages, reminders, phone calls, et cetera. It's also where my mother lists a job for each of us kids, every single day. No matter how busy she is, she always remembers to list daily jobs.

For example, under *Patty* was written: "Don't forget to do my paper route Friday—from Joel." "Fold laundry in dryer—Mom." "Patty is a weeny—from Gess Who."

I had just finished brushing black paint over the *y of* my name and was blowing on it to dry it when Gary Holmes pressed his nose against the side-door glass and nearly scared me out of my wits.

"You try something like that again and you're apt to get black paint across your face," I warned, as I let him in.

Gary set down a huge shopping bag, then sat on the narrow side steps that lead up to the kitchen. He watched as I painted a white *i* where the *y* had been.

"Do you think I should change my name to G-a-r-i?" he asked. "Ooh, I love it. It makes such a statement, don't you think?"

"I think you're for sure going to get black paint across your face if you don't quit making fun and just tell me what you have to talk to me about. You've used up one minute already, so you've got just sixty seconds left."

Gary leaned his elbows back on the step above him, jerked the hair out of his face, and said, "I need your help." I was about to make a smart remark when I saw that he was really serious. I put down my paintbrush and sat next to him. "What's wrong?"

"Oh, don't worry, nothing's wrong. In fact, something great

30

just happened." Gary reached into the shopping bag and pulled out the wooden box that usually sits in the main office at St. Iggie's, the box where students submit entries for *Reflections,* the school's literary magazine.

"Know what this is?" he asked, flipping the padlock on the box.

"Of course I know what it is. I put three entries into it this year already. What the heck did you do—steal it? Are you totally bonkers? Look, if anyone asks, I didn't see you with it. I don't know anything. Now just put it back where you got it and no one will get in any trouble."

I gently took the box away from Gary and tried to put it into the bag. He grabbed it back.

"I didn't steal it. I just brought it over here for show and tell. I'm—"

I cut in and tried to take the box again. "Okay, you showed me you can steal a box out of the office. I'm very impressed. Now tell me you're going to put it right back before you land yourself in detention or get suspended from school."

"I didn't steal the box. Just stifle yourself for a minute so I can make the grand announcement that I'm in charge of this box. I've been chosen this year's editor of *Reflections.*"

We'd been having a tug of war with the box as he spoke. I suddenly let go of my end, sending Gary and the heavy wooden box sprawling on the floor.

"You?" I asked. "Why would they ask you? All you know how to write is graffiti on bathroom walls."

"That's where you're wrong," he said, pulling himself up and putting the box on the step. "I got my start with graffiti, but my real talent is—now don't laugh—poetry."

I started to laugh, till Gary put his hand over my mouth. I bit it.

"I'm not joking," he said, trying to rub the teeth marks off the palm of his hand. "No one knows this but you and Mrs. Nielsen, the literary magazine adviser, but I've been writing poetry for about three years. Some of it got published last year in St. Iggie's magazine, but I asked to be signed Anonymous." He pulled out last year's issue of *Reflections* from inside his jacket and showed me two poems he had written.

"You wrote these?" I could hardly believe it. I had loved one of them so much I had cut it out and put it in my drawer of small important stuff. "I'm sorry I laughed at you. Really, I thought you were joking," I said.

"No, I'm not," he said. He reached into his pocket and pulled out the key to the box as proof.

Then Gary dropped his second bombshell of the afternoon. He asked me if I would be his coeditor.

"You're such a good writer," he said. "I mean, you've got a monthly column in the school newspaper and you always get an A on everything you write in class. Together we'd be awesome. What do you say?"

"Who else would be on the staff?"

"I don't know. An art director and a layout person, probably. And Mrs. Nielsen."

"I'll think about it," I said.

Gary seemed embarrassed as he thanked me. Then he got up abruptly and walked out the side door. Before he closed it he reached over to the blackboard and erased the *y* from the word *weeny*. In its place he put an *i*. Then he jerked the hair out of his eyes, shut the door, and was gone.

I stayed on the step for a while, thinking about what Gary had just asked me to do. As much as I would have loved the honor, no way could I ever agree to it. What if other people saw me sitting with him in the *Reflections* office or saw us working together in the library or talking on the bus? No way would I want anyone to think we were an "item." That would totally blow my chances of getting Tim back. It would also annoy Penni, who seemed to have a low opinion of Gary. No, there was no way I could ever agree to work with Gary Holmes.

That night Tracy called to check on my nail biting. I told her what Gary had asked me to do and confessed that I had sat on the steps biting my nails for about half an hour after he left, thinking about it.

"Why?" Tracy asked. "I can't believe you didn't jump on him and kiss him on the lips for asking you. I mean, coeditor of *Reflections*, wow!"

I explained about Tim and about Penni and about how I just couldn't risk it.

"For Pete's sake," Tracy yelled into the receiver. "It's just Gary."

"Let's drop it," I said.

After we hung up I pulled out my list of resolutions. I put a star in front of number nine—sit near P.P.'s lunch table . . . and number ten—change the spelling of my name to Patti. It wasn't much, but it was a start.

I got into bed and wrote a letter to Fango, including all the questions from the gang at lunch. Then I read the first paragraph of *Great Expectations* before falling off to sleep.

5

Tracy and I stood at the bus stop with our backs to the biting wind. Our feet and various other parts of our bodies were frozen stiff.

"We have to sit near Penni again at lunch today," I told Tracy.

"Why? Didn't you learn your lesson yesterday? Or do you enjoy getting humiliated?" Tracy asked, holding a mittened hand over her mouth and nose to keep them warm.

"I want to apologize to her."

"She's the one who should apologize. She called you clumsy."

"I deserved it. After all, I did squish the air out of her and practically crush her chest."

"You did not deserve it. It was an accident."

"I did too deserve it."

"You did not."

"Did too."

"Did not."

"Look, you're not going to talk me out of it. I'm sitting near her again and you can come or not. But to tell the truth, and don't screech when I say this, you should apologize too, for telling her to go breathe exhaust fumes."

Tracy laughed out loud. "Did you see the look on her face when I said that? I bet no one's ever talked to Penni like that before."

Tracy was hopeless. There was no way I was going to convince her that Penni was my ticket to the cool world and to Tim and I was willing to put up with a little inconvenience for it.

As the bus lumbered into view Gary came sprinting up wearing geeky earmuffs. I couldn't believe my eyes. Didn't he realize no other male at St. Iggie's wore earmuffs? Why didn't he look at himself in the mirror and say, "I look geeky in these things!" and then flush them down the toilet? I mean, frostbite aside, didn't he notice that no guy over the age of six or under the age of sixty on the *entire planet* wears earmuffs?

"Hey, Pattycake," he yelled to me over the roar of the approaching bus, "did you decide yet?"

"No. And don't ever call me Pattycake again, or I'll stuff your earmuffs up your nostrils," I yelled back as I pushed Tracy on the bus ahead of everyone else.

"Watch him bug me every five minutes for my answer," I complained.

"I still can't believe you have to think about it," Tracy said. "Don't take this personally, but sometimes you act like a total moron."

"Let's drop the subject before Gary hears us."

I spent the rest of the ride to school wanting to bite my nails.

At lunch we all sat at the table next to Penni's again. I had to carry my lunch with me all morning and rush like crazy after fourth period to beat the crowd to the cafeteria and reserve the table for us.

I sat across the table this time so I could get a good view of Penni and her friends. They had a lot in common. Every one of them had supershiny hair and all of them had tans, probably from spending Christmas vacation on tropical islands. None of them was overweight, there wasn't a single zit among them, and no one at that table had short, stubby nails like mine. There were no wrinkles in any of their blouses, like mine sometimes has when it sits in the dryer overnight.

The minute Trish sat down at our table she started complaining again about how far we were from the ice cream counter. Tracy smacked her with her brown paper bag to shut her up.

We were just spreading out our lunches, and Kate was trying to convince me that I'd rather have her apple than the Hostess creme-filled cupcakes I had packed in my lunch, when I spotted Gary heading toward our table again, just like the day before. I couldn't believe my eyes. This guy would not give up. I quickly dropped my napkin on the floor and bent down under the table to get it, but I didn't move fast enough. Gary had spotted me and in a few seconds he was crouched down next to me, offering to help find whatever it was I had lost.

"Look," I said, crossing my legs Indian style and turning to face him under the table, "you can't keep following me around like this and asking my decision every five seconds." Gary sat down too and told me he was sorry if he was being a pest. I was glad we were under the table and out of Penni Pendleton's sight, except for the fact that we kept getting kicked and bumped by five sets of legs.

"Okay, look," I said. "Here's the deal. I'd love to work on *Reflections*. But I'm really busy. I've got my column to write, and my baby-sitting job and my homework. Plus my friend Alex is giving me chess lessons. I just can't spare the time."

"Who's Alex?" Gary asked, sounding kind of hurt.

"Just a friend."

"How friendly are you?"

"That's another thing, Gary. If I worked with you, you'd be hanging around me all the time and acting like you own me or something and asking personal questions which are none of your business."

"I'm sorry, Pattyca— I mean Patty. I promise, if you'll be my coeditor I won't even look at you and I'll ask permission before I speak and I won't talk about anything more personal than the weather. Please, Patty, puhl-eez?"

"You're not going to give up, are you? You're going to follow me and keep asking me till I break down. If I hide under the lunch table you're going to follow me. When I go into the girls' john you're going to follow me. When I go to bed at night you're going to climb up the drainpipe and knock on my window and bug me. Right?"

"That's the general idea. I hadn't thought about the drainpipe, but it sounds good. I'll give it a shot." Gary laughed. And I couldn't help myself. I laughed too.

"Hey, what's going on down there?" Tracy asked, sticking her head under the table. "Do you two need a chaperon?"

"No," Gary answered. "I'm just down here checking to see who needs to shave their legs, and yours look worse than my dog's." Tracy kicked him.

Gary turned back to me and said, "Patty, you're forgetting the time we were playing on the football field at Easton College and

37

it started to rain and we went under the bleachers till it stopped. You're forgetting how we promised under those bleachers that we'd always be friends and we'd always be there for each other. We hooked pinkies on it." He held up his little finger for emphasis.

"Do you have to drag that up all the time? We were eight years old, for Pete's sake."

Both of us sat there for a few seconds, not saying anything. I sighed. Gary jerked his head back. Finally I gave in.

"Okay, Gary, I'll do it but on certain conditions. Number one: We do not work at school. We work at my house. Number two: We do not discuss *Reflections* at school. Number three: We do not tell anyone I'm your coeditor. And number four: You throw your earmuffs in the trash. And that rule is for your own good, believe me."

Gary grabbed my hand and hooked our pinkies together. "Deal," he said.

"I forgot rule number five," I added, unhooking our fingers and putting his hand back in his lap. "Under no circumstances are you to touch me."

"You got it, kid. Starting now I wouldn't touch you with a ten-foot pole." Gary crawled out from under the table and walked away.

As I stood up and brushed myself off I noticed Penni staring at me, her eyebrows raised, so I said in a loud voice, "Am I glad that boy came along when he did to help me look for my solid-fourteen-carat-gold charm bracelet that came off my wrist and fell under the table. That boy, whoever he was, saved my life. He found that solid-gold bracelet caught on someone's sock. If I knew his name I would send him a reward."

Tracy yanked me down in my chair and whispered that I should shut my mouth before I started to sound even more stupid than I already did.

I was nervous as I ate my lunch, thinking about how I was going to go over to Penni and apologize for squishing her the day before. My sandwich tasted like cardboard and my cheese curls formed a big mushy lump in my mouth that I could hardly swallow. I decided to give my cupcakes to Kate just so they would get enjoyed.

I was rehearsing what I would say when I saw Penni daintily dab her napkin at the corners of her mouth and give her tray to the girl sitting next to her to be carried to the trash bin.

I jumped up and practically vaulted over the tables to get to her before she left the cafeteria. I tapped her on the shoulder. She turned and looked at me, then looked at the spot where I had touched her.

Quickly, before I lost my nerve, I blurted out, "Hi, Penni, if I can call you Penni, or Penelope, if you'd rather I called you that. My name is Patty, well, Patricia, but you can call me Patty. I mean, if you want to call me anything. Or you can call me anything you like. That is, if you want to ever talk to me. Not that you have to. But if you ever decided to—"

By now Tracy had caught up with me and jabbed me in the ribs. I stopped and took a deep breath. I started over.

"What I want to say is that I'm Datty Pillman, I mean Patty Dillman, and I'm the person who nearly crushed you yesterday and I just wanted to apologize for being stupid."

She looked at me for a few seconds like she was puzzled. Then she said, "Patty Dillman? Are you the one who writes the column for the school paper?"

"Yeah. Why? Did I write something you didn't like? I'm really sorry. Was it the column making fun of sports? I didn't make fun of horseback riding. I would never make fun of a horse. Really. I absolutely love horses. I read *King of the Wind* three times when I was in fifth grade. And when I was ten I used my birthday money to buy a Barbie horse. Or was it—"

Tracy jabbed me again and whispered out of the corner of her mouth, "Ut up shay. You're sounding like an erk jay."

"No," Penni said sweetly as she ran her fingers through her long brown hair. "I love your column. I have difficulty writing. In fact, I'm barely passing English. Daddy says he'll take away my riding lessons if I don't do better."

"I'm glad. I mean, I'm sorry. I mean, I'm glad you like my column but I'm sorry about your riding lessons," I stammered. "Did you know I'm editor of the literary magazine, too?" I blurted out, wanting to impress Penni even more.

"Really? I'd love to have something I wrote published in that. Well, Patty, it was nice to meet you and I accept your apology." Penni waved and glided out of the cafeteria followed by a trail of friends.

"And next time I see you I'll try not to do you any bodily injury," I called after her.

"Wasn't she gorgeous?" I asked Tracy as I threw my garbage into a huge trash can on wheels near the exit. "Did you notice how smooth her skin is? I bet she's never had a zit in her life."

"Ask me if I care," Tracy said, punching her paper bag down hard into the trash barrel.

That night I was at my desk writing my January column for the school paper when Gary called to ask when we could start working on the literary magazine. He told me that he had opened the box of submissions and there was a load of them, and since every English teacher had announced the deadline in class this week, more would be coming in every day.

He suggested we go through and weed out the horrible ones first, then keep narrowing down the choices. We would have to decide on the cover design and work with the layout person on color schemes and artwork. We would have to meet with the printer to talk about deadlines and with Mrs. Nielsen, the adviser. We'd also have to decide if we needed assistants to help us.

Right away I got all excited about the project. I kept thinking about *Reflections* and how Gary and I were going to make it the best issue ever. Maybe it would even win a state award for excellence and we would get a plaque that would be displayed in the trophy case outside the main office in school. I wondered if Gary's and my names would be on it. That could be a problem. But I would deal with it later.

For now, though, I had to get back my concentration and work on my column. I had decided to write about my Christmas vacation and tell all the funny things that happened. I started by telling how Chris got a white mouse for Christmas and played a joke on me by holding it on my pillow right next to my face one morning while I slept. Then he shook me and I woke up to two beady little mouse eyes staring at me. I jumped about three feet into the air, screamed a bloodcurdling scream, and went running all the way out onto the front porch in my nightgown. Actually, the interesting part of the white mouse story was how I had gotten even with Chris, but I wasn't sure if I should include it in the column.

The way I got even was by taking his entire comic book collection and putting it into a grocery bag. I held the grocery bag out my bedroom window and called him up to my room.

"Guess what I'm holding out the window?" I asked him.

41

"Your cootie collection?" he answered, smirking. That was a major mistake. I reached into the bag and showed him one of the comics, his most prized one, a *Superheroes* reunion issue.

He screeched and came at me like a wild man.

"Stop, or I drop them and the snow and wind will put an end to your comic book career," I commanded.

"Mom!" he yelled, not daring to move.

"Mom's not home, tattletale."

"You give those back!"

"Not until you pay for the trick you did on me."

"Okay, okay, what do you want? I'll give you the five dollars Grandma sent me for Christmas."

"Not acceptable."

"I'll give you the five dollars, plus all the change in my bank."

"Not acceptable. I know you just emptied your bank yesterday to buy that dumb wheel for your mouse's cage so he can get his brain scrambled from running around in circles all day."

"What do you want?" Chris squeaked, clenching his fists at his sides to keep from attacking me.

"All I want is a polite apology and a promise to do my days of kitchen cleanup for the rest of Christmas vacation."

"And what if I won't?" he challenged.

"Duh. Then I guess your comic book collection is history." I jiggled the bag out the window.

"All right," he agreed. "Now give me back my comics." Chris grabbed the bag and ran out of my room, yelling back at me, "I had my fingers crossed, weenie." He ran into the bathroom and locked the door.

I stood outside the door and said very quietly, "You'll do what you promised, or little Gus the mouse will pay for it. And another thing—I didn't tell Mom and Dad about what you did to me, so you better not tell them what I did."

After thinking about it for a while I decided not to include my revenge in the column. It made me sound mean, when I'm really not. Mostly, I'm the victim of Chris's bogus tricks, and then when I try to get even I get railed on by my parents for being nasty to him, just because he's younger. It's not fair, and if I ever get reincarnated I want to come back as someone's little brother.

I sat at my typewriter trying to think of anything else interesting that had happened over Christmas and came to the conclusion that nothing had, except for my friend Alex teaching me to play chess and then us going to Ben's Burgers after every lesson. Alex, by the way, is a guy who volunteers at a soup kitchen on Saturdays, like I do. He's cute and nice, but so far there aren't any sparks between us. We just enjoy each other's company.

Tracy called to check on my nail-biting resolution, so I asked her for column ideas, but hers turned out to be as dumb as mine.

In the end I pulled the paper out of my typewriter and crumpled it into the wastebasket. I put on my nightgown, removed the polish from my fingernails and toenails, and repolished them. I did my fingernails hot pink, which is the boldest color we're allowed at St. Iggie's. I did my toenails purple with red polka dots. Then I scrubbed my face. I'd been scrubbing with cleansing granules three times a day since I made my New Year's resolution, but it still wasn't glowing like Penni's. In fact, it seemed like my face was starting to turn blotchy and red. I decided maybe I'd better start scrubbing it four times a day. I got into bed and flipped open *David Copperfield*. After reading the first page I checked the author and, sure enough, it was my buddy Charles Dickens, the guy who took eight lines to finish a sentence. I closed the book and decided to switch authors the next night.

6

Guess who gave me the idea for my January column? Penni
Pendleton!

We were sitting at the lunch table next to hers on Monday
(Trish had finally accepted the fact that this was our new loca-
tion and she would have to hike a few yards to buy her daily fix
of ice cream on a stick).

I was telling the gang how I had wasted the whole weekend
trying to come up with a topic, so they were all throwing ideas
my way. Kate had just suggested that I write about the nicknames we have for different teachers and the reasons behind
them. We were laughing hysterically when Penni turned around
and said, "Excuse me, Patty. I couldn't help overhearing your
conversation and I have an idea for you. Why don't you write
about the ridiculous rules this school has? Honestly, the way

45

they have a rule for everything, it's a wonder we can blow our noses without breaking some precious commandment."

"Gosh, I don't know. It's a great idea, don't get me wrong, and I appreciate your sharing it with me, but I don't want to make trouble," I said, starting to bite my nails.

Penni came over to our table, motioned for Whitney to move out of the chair next to mine, then sat down and went on, "You could be our spokesperson, championing the cause of students' rights. You could even start a committee to meet with the administration to change the rules or else we'd boycott the school. We'd all stand behind you. We'd revolt and you'd be famous—our leader, our crusader!"

"Don't you mean martyr?" Tracy cut in. "Pats, I think Miss Pendleton just wants her gripes publicized with your name attached to them, sparing her any chance of detention, suspension, or black marks on her record."

"That's not true. I just wanted to offer a suggestion that would make Patty a celebrity. But it seems as if she's not ready for it. I'm sorry," Penni huffed. She got up and left.

We were all quiet for a few seconds. Then Trish said, "Anyone want an ice cream while I'm at the counter?"

Kate went back to listing teachers' nicknames, but no one felt like laughing anymore. We finished lunch without saying anything more about Penni's idea.

That night, though, I sat down at my typewriter and worked out a column that I thought might work. It criticized the rules, but I tried to do it in a funny way. I figured I'd show it to Mr. Lampert, the newspaper adviser, and ask his advice. If he gave it the okay I'd not only have my column for the month, I'd also make major points with Penni.

Here's what I wrote:

Susan Wojciechowski

BITS AND PIECES
BY PATRICIA DILLMAN

I love Saint Ignatius. I really do. And I would never speak a word against this school. I really wouldn't. But a lot of the students have been griping about the school rules. I tell them that each and every rule was made only after careful consideration and each one is for the good of the students. But the complaints keep coming and I think it's my duty to bring them to the attention of whoever is IN CHARGE OF RULES. Here's what I've been hearing.

1. Why can't we have coed classes?

2. Why do the girls have to wear knee socks? Knee socks cut off your circulation right below the knee. They leave a red line around your leg that doesn't go away till the middle of summer vacation. And if you break the elastic at the top so your blood can get to your feet, the socks fall down around your ankles and you get yelled at. You end up spending so much time pulling up your socks you miss most of what's being taught in class. There are students who firmly believe that wearing slouch socks, ruffled anklets, and crew socks would raise our class grades.

3. Speaking of socks brings up the subject of shoes. The rules say we have to wear sensible shoes. But some students feel that our uniform shoes bring new meaning to the word "sensible." These shoes are so sensible a cement truck could run over your feet and you wouldn't feel it. Students have developed leg muscles bigger than Arnold Schwarzenegger's from wearing shoes that weigh twenty pounds apiece. Why can't we wear shoes a little less sensible? We promise to stay out of the path of cement trucks.

4. Why can't we have coed classes?

5. Why can't the girls wear eye makeup to school? Certain students, not including myself of course, feel that eye makeup would make us look more mature, which would cause us to act more mature, which is what the teachers are always telling us to do.

6. When will the girls' gym uniforms be updated? Some students think that ours look like bathing suits out of the eighteenth century. Again, I do not share that opinion. I feel the suits are designed to fit the growing girl so our parents won't have to buy new ones every time we gain 100 pounds.

7. Why can't we have coed classes?

8. Cafeteria food. Why do the burgers taste like plastic? What is the purpose of those little red, rubbery bits of stuff mixed in with all the vegetables? Why aren't students allowed to leave the school grounds during lunch periods so they can eat at McDonald's or Burger King and enjoy french fries that don't look and taste like rubber bands?

Now that I've told you the criticisms of some of the students, I'd like to say, in case I haven't mentioned it already, that I personally find nothing to complain about. I feel Saint Ignatius is the best— Excuse me a minute while I pull up my socks—As I was saying, Saint Ignatius is the best school in the county and provides us with a high-quality— Excuse me again, I just got a cramp in my leg muscle. Nothing to worry about. It happens all the time. A little rubbing and it'll be as good as new—a high-quality education which will prepare us for— Could you hold on one second while I get a toothpick? There's a piece of red stuff between my teeth—will prepare us for any challenge the world may present.

After I read the column over I started to get nervous wondering what Penni would think of it. I can't believe I did this, but I even called her on the phone to read her the column and ask her opinion of it. I practically hyperventilated as I dialed her number and I was so scared that my voice came out sounding like I had inhaled from a helium balloon. You know how it is when you have to make a call that you're scared to make, like when you're calling a boy to ask him to a dance or something. First you hope someone will be using your phone so you can put it off and be in agony for a while longer. Then you hope the other person's line will be busy. Then you hope they're not home.

Well, that's the way it went when I decided to call Penni. But in the end, I did it.

As I read her the column she laughed out loud and said she loved it.

"Patty, you are so talented. I'm jealous," she said in her smooth, throaty voice.

"Really?" I squeaked.

"Really. You're so good I think you could write a research paper in one night if you wanted to."

"Really?" I squeaked again and wished I could get my voice back to normal. I started biting my nails, then yanked them out of my mouth.

"Really," Penni said. "Now I'm the opposite. I have a paper due in a week and I can't even get started. I have no writing ability whatsoever. Do you have any helpful hints?"

"Well, I usually try for a good opening and a good closing and try to get away with putting a little garbage in between. I figure if the teacher is loaded down with papers, maybe she just reads beginnings and endings and skims the rest." This was the most

I had ever said to Penni in one breath and I was totally hyper-ventilating. I started biting my nails big-time, New Year's resolution or not.

"That's very helpful, Patty."

"Really?"

"Really. Patty, I've been meaning to ask you something. Would you like to come to a party at my house next Saturday?"

"Me? Party? Your house? Saturday?" I knew I was talking like a dweeb, but my mind couldn't completely grasp what was happening.

"That's one hundred percent right." Penni laughed. "You. Party. My house. Saturday. Can you come? It'll be so much fun!"

Just as I was trying to form the word "yes" Penni's voice turned into a whine. "Oh, wait a minute. Never mind. Forget I even asked. I just remembered my father told me I can't have a party till my research paper is finished. It was going to be an awesome party too. I was going to invite the whole football team."

Without thinking about it I blurted, "No problem. Why don't I help you with the paper some night this week?"

"Really?" Penni said, and giggled.

"Really," I answered. The thought crossed my mind that I might be taking on more than I could handle. But Tim would be at the party and I would get to put a star next to resolution number eleven—get invited to parties at P.P.'s. It was worth it.

We agreed that I'd help her on Tuesday night at her house and the party would be on for Saturday. Penni even told me I could invite a friend.

I hung up the phone, made a fist in the air, and yelled "Yes!" at the top of my lungs. Then I called Tracy to tell her about the miracle that had just happened.

Tracy didn't sound the least bit excited. All she kept saying was, "You read Penni the column before me? You always read me your columns first."

"Look, forget the column," I explained patiently. "The column is not the main idea of this conversation. The main idea is that I can die now because one of my greatest goals in life has been fulfilled. I have been invited to a Pendleton party."

"Whoop de doo. Just think, you'll get to hear how much Penni's latest outfit cost, which remote Caribbean island she went to over Christmas, and gosh, maybe you'll even get to discuss the high cost of good caviar these days. Could I ask you to take notes so you can share every moment with me after it's over?"

"Won't have to. You're invited too."

"Darn, I can't make it. I have to deflea my dog that night."

When I told her the whole football team, including Scott Wandover, was invited she started to soften. In the end she said she'd have to come, just to make sure I didn't make a complete turkey out of myself. I said I appreciated her special knack for building up a person's self-esteem.

"Hey, before next Saturday could you come over and straighten my hair?" I asked Tracy.

"Oh no. You're not going to try to look like Princess Penni, are you?"

"No," I fibbed. "You know I've wanted to straighten my hair for at least a kajillion years."

"I bet you haven't told your mom yet, have you? She's gonna spazz royally. I bet you any money she'll give you the speech about how your curly hair is a God-given gift and anyone would give their eyeteeth for those curls and your hair is your crowning glory, blah, blah, blah. I bet she won't let you do it."

"Leave it to me. Just hold Thursday night open, okay?"

51

PROMISES TO KEEP

"I'll hold it open, but I bet I spend the evening sitting home listening to my mother tell me to practice my trumpet."

After we hung up I went in search of Mom. I found her in the kitchen folding laundry, so I sat down at the table and casually asked her if she'd pick up a hair-straightening kit the next time she was at the store.

Mom motioned for me to help with the laundry as she launched into her speech.

"I hope you aren't planning to use it on yourself," she said, raising her eyebrows. Who did she think I was planning to use it on—Chris's white mouse?

"Yeah, sort of," I mumbled.

"Listen, young lady, that curly hair of yours is a God-given gift and you should be thankful for it. Anyone else would give their eyeteeth for curly hair. Now I know that right now you consider your hair a curse, but believe me, it's beautiful, your crowning glory," she said as she shook out a pair of jeans so hard they made a snapping sound.

I called Tracy and told her to cancel Thursday. "Well, actually it's just a postponement," I corrected myself. "I'll keep working on Mom till I wear her down. And by the way, don't even ask whether I got through today without biting my nails. I bit them down to stubs while I was on the phone with Penni and it was worth it."

That night I tried, really tried, to read a whole page of a World's Greatest Classic. This time it was Chaucer's *Canterbury Tales,* and I'm sorry, but the person who put together the World's Greatest Classics list must have been playing some kind of joke or done it on a dare. The only thing these books are good for is to cure insomnia.

52

I quit reading and, instead, made my own list of the World's Greatest Classics:

1. *Everything You Always Wanted to Know About Boys but Were Afraid to Ask*
2. *Calvin and Hobbes,* all volumes
3. anything by Stephen King
4. *The Junior Miss Book of Makeup Magic*
5. *1001 Hairstyles*
6. *The Guinness Book of World Records*
7. *Garfield Goes Hollywood*

When I got into bed I couldn't relax. I kept thinking about what Penni's party would be like and how I could get my hands on some money fast so I could buy a leather skirt. I thought about seeing Tim, and trying to make conversation with Penni's classy friends. I wished I had a tan, long nails, shiny hair, a cashmere sweater—anything to make me feel like I would fit in at the party. My mind started to spin. I finally had to read another paragraph of *The Canterbury Tales* just to get to sleep.

7

I was nervous going to Penni's house to help her with her social studies paper. First of all, she lives in a really exclusive section of Easton. It made me feel jittery just to know I was actually going to walk into one of those awesome homes. Second, I wondered if I was dressed okay. Before we left I changed my outfit three times. I even made Dad change out of his "I Spotted Elvis" sweatshirt and put on something more appropriate, even though he was just dropping me off. Third, I wondered what Penni's parents would be like. Fourth, I worried whether I'd act right and say the right things, or make a complete horse's rear out of myself.

To calm my nerves, I reread the note Penni had stuck through my locker vents that morning.

It was on yellow parchment paper with a ruffly edge at the

bottom. Penni's name and address were engraved at the top. The note was typed and it said:

Don't forget about tonight. I know you can give me some good advice about my paper. You are such a talented writer.

I can't wait for Saturday. What we are going to do at the party: dance, listen to music, play games, watch videos.

Who is coming: everyone who matters.

Food: pizza, tacos, choose-your-own-toppings sundaes.

It was signed in Penni's gorgeous handwriting:

Luv 'N' Stuff
Penni

When we reached the Pendletons' house Dad asked me if I got the address right. It looked like some kind of castle. Surrounding the house was a lawn big enough to be a national park. And around that was a stone wall with an iron gate at the entrance, only it looked like the iron gate was always kept open, because there were shrubs planted along the base of it on both sides. You went up this long U-shaped driveway that curved around at the front door to the castle and then went back to the road. The door itself was enormous and was stained, not painted, and had big black hinges across it.

Dad let out a long, slow whistle as he stopped the car.

"Shall I come 'round and escort you to the door, miss?" he asked.

"No, Jeeves, that will be all for tonight. And please, see to it that you use the Porsche in the future."

I licked my lips and wiped the palms of my hands down my jeans before I rang the bell. Our bell at home goes *ding-dong*. Or sometimes *ding-buzz,* 'cause there's an electrical short in it. This one played half a symphony. The guy who drives Penni to school answered it and let me into a foyer as big as our living room. The floor was covered with big black and white tiles, and while I waited for Penni I tried to imagine a giant chess game being played on it. Penni came down and took me up a staircase (curved, and with a gleaming wood banister like in the movies) to her room.

I don't even want to talk about her room. It makes me sick just to compare it to mine. My whole room could be her closet. In fact, she had so many clothes she needed a closet as big as my room. Really, I don't even want to talk about her room. Let me just say I literally drooled when I stepped inside. It had white, carved wood furniture and a queen-size bed covered with about a jillion little ruffled pillows. Everything was done in little yellow flowers: the wallpaper, the drapes, the comforter, the dust ruffle, the pillows, the window seat cushion, even a stuffed cat. Honestly, that room made me so jealous I don't want to talk about it anymore, except to say that it reminded me of a room I saw on *Lifestyles of the Rich and Famous* where they showed a movie star's house. The teenage daughter's room made me just about die with envy. That's how Penni's room was. I don't even want to talk about it.

Penni sat down on the window seat, where she had some books and papers scattered around.

"Here's the ammunition," she said. "What can you do with it?"

There wasn't much ammunition. She had only a few notes, and the books were two encyclopedia volumes.

"What's the paper supposed to be about?" I asked.

"We're to choose the three discoveries or inventions that we feel had the greatest impact on society during the twentieth century and explain why," she said.

"What three did you choose?"

"Well, actually I hadn't narrowed it down to three yet."

"How many did you narrow it down to?"

"Well, actually all I did was start to look things up in the encyclopedia."

Penni sat flipping the pages of a volume of *The Encyclopedia Britannica*. Finally she asked me which three inventions I would choose.

"Well, personally I think the greatest invention of the century is Cool Ranch Doritos. And I'd give second place to that nail polish remover where you just dip your finger in the jar. Those two discoveries have made my life worth living."

I started to laugh, but Penni just gave me a dirty look and said, "This is no time for jokes. We've got a paper to write and you told me you'd help. If I don't get to have that party Saturday it'll be all your fault." She stood up and folded her arms across her chest.

I apologized to Penni. I figured she was one of those people who don't have much of a sense of humor, and besides, it wasn't fair of me to be making fun of her paper when she was having a mental block with it. I suggested we haul ourselves over to the public library and get busy.

James drove us. When we got there Penni acted like she'd

never been in a library before. I had to look up all the books and pull them off the shelves. Then she just kind of leafed through them while I took all the notes. When I suggested she check some books out she told me she didn't have a library card yet. So I ended up putting them on my card. I was getting a little ticked at her, but I kept reminding myself about the party and Tim and I managed to keep my mouth shut.

Back at her house I sat down at the typewriter and did an opening paragraph. Meanwhile she was supposed to come up with three inventions. When I finished I went over to the window seat and looked at her notebook. She hadn't written down a thing.

"Patty, I'm sorry. I just can't think," she apologized. "I'm so nervous about this paper my brain won't work. Do you ever get like that, where your mind just freezes up? Maybe if we talk about ideas, things will start to click."

So we talked. Every time I suggested something, Penni said that was exactly what she was thinking. She told me our minds must be on the same wavelength and she had the feeling we were going to be great friends.

I called Mom and asked if I could come home later than I had planned; it was an emergency.

"What exactly is this emergency?" Mom wanted to know. "I hope you're not watching MTV or some totally objectionable movie on cable, Patty."

Honestly, my mother is the most suspicious person in the entire cosmos. I assured her that the emergency was of the homework variety. She agreed to let me stay, but her voice sounded like she intended to find out more about the whole Penni Pendleton situation.

At eleven-fifteen I got up from Penni's desk. My fingers were numb, my brain was numb, but a rough draft of the paper was done.

Penni hugged me and told me how great we work together. She said her father's secretary would polish up the paper and retype it. She must have been so tired she forgot to thank me for practically writing the whole thing myself.

While we waited for James to bring the car around to the front door I asked Penni where her parents were.

"Oh, Father's in Switzerland on business and Mother went with him."

"Do you have the whole house to yourself, or do you have any brothers or sisters?"

"Just me."

"Wow, that's totally awesome. You can stay up late and eat all kinds of junk and leave the dishes till five minutes before they get home and not do your jobs every day. Man, I wish my parents would even go to the next county overnight."

Penni didn't answer; she just shrugged her shoulders and walked me to the door. Her pink leather flats, which matched her sweater perfectly, echoed in the huge foyer.

"See you Saturday," I said as I got into the front seat of the Mercedes James had pulled up to the door.

"That's right, I invited you to the party."

"And I'm bringing a friend. Remember, you told me I could," I added.

"Yes, I did, didn't I? Who are you bringing? Not that pathetic boy who keeps trailing after you all the time, I hope. Oh, I'm sorry. He's not your boyfriend, is he?"

"No way. I hardly know him. I'm bringing Tracy Gilmore. She's the girl who was with me that day I apologized for crushing you."

"I remember. Well, if that's who you want to bring, I'll see you and Stacy about seven-thirty. Toodles."

"Toodles," I answered as the car glided away. I stuck my head out the window and yelled back into the wind, "Not Stacy—Tracy."

James drove me home in silence. I was so tired I didn't even wash my face or give my hair a hundred strokes. I just flopped onto the bed fully clothed.

I couldn't get to sleep, though. I lay there thinking about how I had written Penni's paper for her and trying to convince myself not to feel guilty about it. It was after three when I finally fell into a fitful sleep of tossing and turning and dreaming that I was in a prison cell and my head kept banging against the toilet.

8

On Wednesday I was so tired I fell asleep during one of my classes. That's something I've never done before, no matter how boring a class is—and believe me, I've been in some boring ones.

My eyelids chose to give up right in the middle of Sister Clarabelle's religion class, the worst possible choice. I mean, that nun sees everything and she doesn't let anything go by her. Couldn't she just let me sleep? Couldn't she decide that maybe I was up all night studying or being sick to my stomach or something? Couldn't she pretend she didn't see, like some teachers do when kids pull something mildly annoying?

I remember one time when Laura Limperopoulis started rolling jawbreakers up the aisle of Mrs. Brewer's math class. You could hear them rolling softly along, one by one, till they hit the front wall. But did Mrs. Brewer make a scene? No. She just kept on teaching like nothing happened, and Laura finally stopped.

Not Sister Clarabelle. No way. Instead she yelled, "Patricia!" in her meanest "teacher" voice, which made me jump about a mile out of my seat and knock my religion book off my desk. For a minute I didn't know where I was. All I knew was that drool was running out of the side of my mouth and everyone was looking at me, smiling.

Then Sister C. switched to a real soft voice and said, "I'm sorry I had to wake you, but I was finding it difficult to project over the decibel level of your snoring."

Of course, right then and there my head started to pound from getting awakened in such a rude way and from knowing I'd been drooling and snoring in front of the whole class. I had a headache the rest of the day.

The headache got worse at lunch when Gary came waltzing over to our table again. It was getting to be a ritual with him.

"What am I, some kind of magnet?" I asked him. "Can't you deliver your messages to me by mail?"

"I just want to set a date for us to work on *Reflections*," Gary apologized.

"Don't use the word 'date' when you're talking to me in public."

"Okay, I just want to settle this affair before it's too late," he answered, grinning. He said the word "affair" real loud. I raised my chair up a few inches and smashed it down on his foot.

"I free your foot when you agree to whisper," I said, grinning back at him.

"Okay, okay," he whispered through gritted teeth. I lifted the chair. "Man, you're determined to destroy my feet one way or another. What did they ever do to you?"

To get rid of him, I said he could come to my house that night to work. When he left the table, hobbling on one foot, Penni turned around and told me I should buy some nerd repellent. I laughed, but my face was beet red.

I stuffed my used waxed paper and napkin into my lunch bag, wondering if Gary would ever stop embarrassing me.

"Hey, I got another letter from Fango," I announced to the gang. I dredged it out of my purse and read it out loud. Here's what Fango wrote:

Dear Patty,

Thanks for writing back. No it didnt hurt my feelings that your writing to get extra credit in school. Im glad you told me so I know how honest you are.

Thanks for telling me about your famly. I had a little brother that was a pest too. Your dad must be smart to be head of the english dept at a college. Dont show him my letters. He would bust a gut if he saw how I write.

I taped that list of all your friends questions to my wall and I will answer them all, but not all in one letter.

You asked what we wear. Well, we can wear diffrent pants but we got to wear shirts with our number on the back. The number tells where were from and what our crime is and what year we come in and where our cell is located. The guards always call you by your number, never your name. Were not allowed to wear anything blue, because thats what color the guards wear and I guess they dont want to mistake us for guards. Ha-ha.

PROMISES TO KEEP

You asked how I spend my day. At 7 am we get counted. A bell rings and we got to stand near our cell door till the guard counts us. If your not standing up you get written up, which means you get a punishment which means you could spend a few days in the box which is a cell with hardly nothing in it and you dont leave it at all.

One time Bobo in the next cell didnt stand up for count. So the next thing I hear is noises like things hiting the wall and they drag him away and I dont see Bobo for a week and after he come back he stood up every time for the count.

8 oclock is brekfast. We line up outside our cells and march two by two to the mess hall. No talking allowed. If the guard wants us to stop he hits on the wall twice with his club. If he wants us to start walking he hits it once. Theres no talking at meals ether. Brekfast is ok cause its cold sereal, but lunch and supper are sometimes not worth the walk. I work all morning making licents plates. Maybe the licents plate on your car was made by me. I hope it looks good. Ha-ha.

Then we go back to our cells, then head count again, then lunch, then back to work, back to cell, head count, supper.

At night we watch tv which is outside in the cortyard—no one watches much tv in the winter unless you put on your long underwear and coat and gloves. Sometimes we play basketball at night or go to classes or just lay around in the cell doing nothing. I draw or paint every chance I get. Next letter I will send you something I painted.

We are allowed a shower 2x a week. My days are Tuseday and Thursday. Other then that we wash off in our sink, we call that a bird bath.

Patty, you are probly saying to yourself that this does not sound like life in the fast lane and you are right. I never even got one vister in the 4 years I been here. One time my sister took a six hour bus ride to visit me. I tell her ahead that you need two forms of ID to get in so she brought two and they told her one of them was no good so they wouldnt let her see me. A guard told me this and I cried. My sister told me she stood outside the gate and cried.

Patty, it is time for lights out so I got to end this letter. Tell me what your taking in school. Tell me more about your friends. Tell them thanks for the questions. If you send me your picture I will draw it.

Answer to last riddle—leaves

New riddle—What can you put in a barrel to make it lighter?

Here is a trivial question—How much water does a person use every day to brush his teeth?

from
Fango

PS There are no curtins in front of the toilets. This isnt no Holiday In.

"Man, prison sounds a lot like St. Iggie's," Tracy said.

"Yeah," Kate said, "only the inmates broke a law to get there. We're just innocent kids."

"Well, all I have to say is that I will never break a single law as long as I live. I would just die if I had to go to prison and only take two showers a week," Whitney added, holding her nose.

"Did you tell him what I told you to put in your letter?" Trish wanted to know. "You know, the helpful hint about how if some-one sneaks up and grabs you you can push their nose up into their brain?"

"I'm sure he knows all those helpful hints, Trish. The guy is a convicted armed bank robber, for Pete's sake. He's not in the slammer for having too many parking tickets," Tracy said, and hit Trish with her lunch bag.

Everyone was making guesses at how much water it takes to brush your teeth, when I looked at my watch. "Hey, I've got to run," I told everyone. "I have to help Mr. Lampert lay out copy for the newspaper before my next class." I folded the letter and slid it back into my purse.

Whitney leaned toward me and asked quietly, "That reminds me—what did you finally decide to write about in your column?"

"Dumb school rules, like Penni suggested," I answered loud enough for Penni to hear. "Well, gotta go. Toodles!" I waved and sidestepped between the chairs.

As I got to the aisle I heard Tracy saying to everybody at our table, "Toodles? Did I hear her say 'toodles'? Tell me I heard wrong. Please, somebody tell me she said something about eating Cheez Doodles, or that she's getting a poodle. Tell me she didn't say 'toodles' or I'm going to be sick." I knew Penni could hear every word. I wondered if maybe it wasn't such a good idea after all to be sitting at a table near Penni's.

That night Gary showed up with a stack of submissions a mile high. At our school everyone wants to get something printed in *Reflections*, so they submit poems, essays, and short stories from September right up to the deadline. It's a big honor and at the annual awards assembly in June all the kids who made it into *Reflections* get a certificate. Also, the magazine is in a statewide competition and two people who've gotten something published get picked to go to the banquet along with the editors. It's usually in some other city.

"See why I wanted us to get busy?" Gary said as he dumped the papers on the kitchen table. He threw his jacket at me and I could see that he was wearing his usual outfit of jeans and a short-sleeved, plaid shirt with a button-down collar. He wears short-sleeved, plaid shirts all the time, even if it's ten degrees below zero.

From the kitchen he bellowed, "Hi, Mr. Dillman. Hi, Mrs. Dillman, wherever you are!" Mom answered hi from upstairs and Dad came in to say hi and to thank Gary for helping push his car out of a snowbank where it had skidded the day before.

Then Gary bellowed, "Hi, Joel. Hi, Chris. Hi, Mary, wherever you are!" And from various parts of the house came "Yo, Gar! How's it going?" "Hi, Gary," and "Can you come up and see me on the big potty?" Gary laughed.

"What do you say we go up to your room and get started?" he said, jabbing me in the ribs. "If you know what I mean."

I gave him my dirtiest look. "Come on, cut the cute remarks. There's no one around to impress but me, and it's way too late for any hope there. So just get serious and we can get some work done, okay?" Gary jerked his hair out of his face twice.

"We can work in here," I went on. "The kitchen table's the best place to spread things out—as long as you don't mind people and other forms of life walking in and out all night."

I had no sooner said the words than Chris walked in chanting, "H-o-m-o-g-e-n-i-z-e-d, h-o-m-o-g-e-n-i-z-e-d."

"See what I mean about the other forms of life? This is our

67

family robot. He speaks in code, only his computer chip is stuck on *homogenized.*"

Gary gave Chris a thumbs-up sign and said, "This looks like a kid who just learned how to spell one of the hardest words in the English language. Way to go, sport." They gave each other a high five and a low five. Chris walked out grinning like an idiot and chanting, "H-o-m-o-g-e-n-i-z-e-d, h-o-m-o-n-o-m-o-n-o-g-e-n-i-z-e-d."

"Hey, Einstein," I started to call after him, "you sp—" But before I could finish telling Chris he spelled it wrong Gary touched my arm and put his finger to his lips for me to shut up.

"I remember when I first learned how to spell Tallahassee," he said. "I was on top of the world for a week. Why spoil Chris's fun?"

"You're right," I answered. "You know what my moment of glory was? The word *diarrhea.* And I won't even tell you the trick I used to remember it has two *r*s."

All evening, every time Chris walked by the room spelling *homogenized,* Gary would give him a thumbs-up sign and Chris would grin.

Gary and I read poems till our eyes blurred. It seemed like every kid in school, whether the kid could write poetry or not, had turned in a bunch of them. Most of the time Gary and I groaned after the first few lines and put the poem in our "loser" pile. But once in a while there'd be a gem and the one who had it would stand up and read it as if to an audience. Then if the other agreed we'd put it in our "YES!" pile.

Some of them we'd argue over. One of us would love a particular poem and the other would make a gagging motion. So we put those in our "to be continued" pile.

"Here's a good one," Gary said. "Listen."

> Things I Fear
> I fear falling grades
> and wet parades.
> Unfriendly smiles
> and fierce crocodiles.
>
> I fear dentist chairs
> and falling tears.
> Losing friends
> and fading trends.
>
> I fear frogs and toads
> and going home on foggy roads.
> Family fights
> and filthy sights.
>
> I fear wild fires
> and flat tires.
> Being late for mass
> and forgetting class.
>
> All these fears I feel
> will disappear some night
> and be replaced I fear
> with fewer, but different frights.

"That was nice," I said when he'd finished. "It gives you something to think about. If kids read it in *Reflections* it might get them started thinking about things they're afraid of."

"Such as?" Gary asked.

"Such as it's none of your business what I'm afraid of."

"Come on, be a sport."

PROMISES TO KEEP

"Okay, you asked for it." I thought for a few seconds, then said, "I'm afraid of flunking a subject, having a blob of mayonnaise or mustard on my chin and nobody telling me, going blind, going upstairs to the bathroom at my grandmother's house—I still think there's a monster living in her spare bedroom—not having a date for the spring dance, forgetting to take a price tag off a piece of clothing before I wear it, getting one of those diseases that make you end up in a wheelchair—stop me if you've heard enough, Gary—making a fool of myself by saying something dumb, being a nerd, tripping when I walk and there are boys around, getting a whole colony of zits at once, having the shoplifter alarm go off when I leave a store even though I didn't shoplift anything—stop me, please—spitting when I talk, nuclear annihilation, dying, the people who make Pepsi going on strike, pollution, having a demented chain saw murderer break into my house at night and being so scared I can't even scream—stop me, I mean it—having my hair cut and having it come out awful, getting hit in the face with a soccer ball in gym, making a speech in front of an audience, having my diary get into the wrong hands—"

Finally Gary put his hand over my mouth. "You sound like a real together kind of person. Did your parents store you in a dark closet for a few years, or what?"

"How about you, Gary? What are your fears?"

"My biggest fear is a fear of telling anyone my fears."

"Not acceptable. Come on, I told you tons. The least you can do is tell me one horrible, terrible, embarrassing fear."

"Okay. One fear. Let's see. I've got a fear of having all my shoes stolen, except for my tiger slippers."

We both laughed. "Do you forgive Tracy and me for doing that?" I asked.

70

"No way. Some night I'm going to come up to your room with a chain saw and you'll be so scared you won't be able to scream."

"Not to worry. With your style, you won't be able to get the motor started."

Gary looked at his watch. "It's getting late. I'd love to stick around and listen to a few hundred more of your fears, but I think I should shove off so you can get your beauty sleep. God knows, you need it."

"Har-har. You're no prize yourself. I hear you were so ugly as a baby your mother used to put your hat on backward when she took you out for a walk in your buggy."

We decided to work for fifteen more minutes. We read silently for a while till Gary found another poem he liked. "Here's one that reminds me of Penni Pendleton," he said, and read it aloud.

Standing Alone
I saw her standing there
all alone with no one to hold her
her eyes glowed with the blue from the sky
her hair shined like gold from the sun
But what caught my eye the most
was that she
the prettiest of all
stood alone with no one to love her
but herself

"What do you mean, it reminds you of Penni?" I demanded. "Penni has lots of friends."

"Yeah," Gary said. "Real true-blue ones."

"She does, and I'm one of them. I even got invited to a party at her house this Saturday," I bragged.

"What did you have to pay for the invitation?"

"You're just jealous, Gary Holmes. Sometimes you get me so mad."

Gary didn't answer. He just put the poem in the "YES!" pile without even asking my opinion. I sat there steaming for a few minutes, till Gary said he was sorry he hurt my feelings.

When it was time to go Gary put the papers into folders. I walked him to the front door and stood there not saying anything. I was suddenly feeling tongue-tied. I don't know why. Gary was, too.

"Well, 'bye. It was fun," he said. He reached into his pocket and took out his earmuffs, then put them back.

"Yeah, it was fun."

Gary jerked his hair out of his eyes and walked into the darkness.

When I went upstairs and passed Chris's room I could hear him quietly spelling *homogenized* in bed. I stuck my head in the doorway and told him how awesome it was that he could do it. I told him I couldn't spell *homogenized* till I was ten.

"Why are you being nice to me?" he asked suspiciously. "Is this some kind of trick?"

I came in and sat at the end of his bed. "Come on. Give me a break," I said. "Can't I say something nice without you getting all hyper?" I leaned toward him to tousle his hair, but he pulled back, so I missed.

"I'm telling," he said.

"Telling what? That I'm being nice to you? That I gave you a compliment? Oh, please don't. I don't want to get grounded."

Chris looked at me for a few seconds like he was trying to figure out what the heck was going on. Finally he smiled and said, "Tomorrow I'm going to start practicing the word *hippo-*

potamus. Then I'm going to spell them both for show and tell."

"That ought to blow everybody right out of the water. Well, get to sleep now. 'Night."

"Gary's nice," Chris said as he snuggled under the covers.

"All that spelling has put your brain out of commission. You better get to sleep fast, before you say anything else crazy." I tucked Chris's stuffed tiger under the covers with him and went to my room.

I dug Gary's poem from last year's *Reflections* out of my drawer of small important stuff and read it again. Then I scrubbed my face and got into bed. I didn't even attempt reading any of the World's Greatest Classics. I was tired enough already. That night I slept like a rock. I didn't toss or turn or dream of being in a prison cell with my head hitting the toilet.

9

Gary didn't stop by my lunch table the rest of the week. He walked by but just kept on going. I guess he finally got the message.

Each time he came into sight Penni would motion to me from the next table and warn me that he was coming, by saying stuff like "Geek alert" or "Nerd alert." Then she and her friends would laugh, but no one from our table laughed. I wondered if Gary, or the friends he was with, heard.

On Friday Penni came to my table to tell me she had handed in her paper and it looked fantastic. She said she had a copy to show her father when he came home from his trip that night. She was all excited about how proud he'd be.

"That's nice," I mumbled, and changed the subject. I asked her what time the party was and what everyone would be wearing.

When Penni left, Tracy asked me why she'd reported to me about her paper.

"I kind of helped her edit it," I said.

"When?"

"A few nights ago."

"How come you didn't tell me?"

"I didn't think you'd care to know. What is this, a federal investigation? Do I have to tell you every move I make? Are you my mother?" I stuffed the rest of my sandwich into my lunch bag, got up, and left.

"What's her problem?" I heard Tracy say as I stomped away. "She didn't even say toodles."

On the bus ride home I apologized to Tracy.

"I guess I feel kind of guilty for helping Penni with her paper," I explained.

"Why? We help each other with homework."

"Well, to tell you the truth, I sort of wrote it for her. I don't know how it happened. I didn't mean to, but before I knew it I was doing the whole thing. All she did the whole night was sit around running her fingers through her hair."

"Well, it's over and done with, so don't keep kicking yourself. Maybe Penni is just the type of person who uses people, so you've got to watch out for yourself."

"What do you mean 'uses people'?" I said, so sharply that Tracy jumped slightly in her seat. "She didn't use me. I did it of my own free will. I'm the one who suggested going to her house to help her. I'm the one who called my parents to ask if I could stay later to work. I'm the one who hit the typewriter keys. She didn't exactly hold a gun to my head."

"Sorry I said anything. I didn't know you were so touchy about this."

I didn't answer. And for the rest of the ride I sat silently biting my nails. Tracy didn't even jab me with her elbow to remind me to stop.

I didn't admit it to Tracy, but I was surprised too at my sudden outburst when Tracy criticized Penni. Ever since Tuesday I had been angry with myself and with Penni because I felt like I'd been tricked, and now I was suddenly defending her. The only thing I knew was that I wanted to like Penni and to be friends with her so much, and I wanted Tracy to like her too.

The school bus belched to a stop in front of the Easton campus. Tracy and I got off and started walking in opposite directions. After a few steps, though, we both turned around and said, "Sorry" at the same time. We grinned at each other.

"I'll call you when I get home," Tracy said.

When I got home I took the phone into the hall closet and settled on the floor with it in my lap.

The phone rang. I picked it up and began rattling on about how sorry I was for acting like a dweeb on the bus. "Forgive me?" I asked.

"I forgive you, Patty, and for your penance you will remember to come in for a filling tomorrow at four-thirty," answered a woman's laughing voice.

I nearly died of embarrassment when I realized it was Fran, the receptionist at my dentist's office.

"Tomorrow?" I groaned, realizing Penni's party was tomorrow, too.

"Yes," said Fran.

"Cavity filling?" I asked, feeling my heart sink.

"Right."

"Four-thirty?"

"Correct. See you then." She hung up before I had a chance to tell her about how I couldn't possibly come because of the party.

The phone rang again. This time it was Tracy. "Can't talk now. Emergency. Call you later," I said hurriedly, and hung up without waiting for an answer.

"Mom," I called out, replacing the phone on the hall table. "Mommm!" I turned around and bumped into my mother.

"Look," I explained, "I've got a problem. I forgot I had a dentist appointment tomorrow. I'll go any other day of the year, but I simply cannot go tomorrow. Dr. Rosen'll stretch out my whole mouth and my lips will be swollen and beet red for Penni's party. Or worse yet, he'll give me Novocaine and one side of my mouth will be hanging down to my chin and drool will be running out and I won't even feel it for the next six hours. I absolutely can't go, not the day of the party. Please, Mom?"

"I'm sorry, but you made that appointment yourself when you had your teeth cleaned last month," Mom said in that level, calm voice she uses when I'm about to go totally hyper. "You're blowing this all out of proportion. You're going and there will be no further discussion about it."

I swear my mother was never a teenager. I went to my dad's den where he was correcting a stack of papers from his Introduction to Composition course. "Dad, do you have any cavities that need filling?"

"Why? Are you taking a dentistry course through the mail?"

"No. I'm looking for someone to take my place at Dr. Rosen's tomorrow."

"Sorry to disappoint you, but my teeth are in good shape at the moment."

"Darn."

I went back to Mom. "Doesn't Joel or Chris or Mary have any cavities that need filling?"

"Joel and Chris went to the dentist last week, and Mary isn't old enough to go yet."

"Not old enough? Not old enough? She's three, for Pete's sake! The kid's mouth could be festering with disease. She could have cavities in her mouth that are working their way into her jawbones as we speak. What kind of mother are you? Get her to that office before she gets gingivitis or pyorrhea or one of those horrible diseases you read about in the pamphlets in Dr. Rosen's waiting room." I grabbed Mary off the floor, where she was playing with an old Barbie of mine whose head was missing. I pried my sister's mouth open, looking for signs of decay. She bit my finger.

"Oh great, now I'll have a swollen finger for the party on top of everything else. I may as well just stay home."

"That's up to you," Mom said calmly. "But you are going to the dentist."

I went into the hall closet to call Tracy and complain about my unreasonable mother. Tracy understood completely.

"One time when I was in sixth grade," she told me, "my mother had some friends over and she made me show them a rash I had on my stomach and lower back, and I do mean *lower* back. I told her I didn't want to, but she said, 'What are you embarrassed about? We're all women,' and she made me show them. I wanted to die."

When Tracy and I finally finished complaining about our mothers, and finished apologizing for how we'd acted on the bus, I warned her not to dare call me at bedtime to ask how my nail-biting resolution was going, because I knew for sure it wouldn't be going too well. Then she wished me luck at the dentist and we hung up.

That night I scrubbed my face extra hard with cleansing granules, just in case by some miracle I would be able to show my face at the party. Then I glued on a set of fake nails, but two of them fell off as I was brushing my hair three hundred strokes.

10

I was right. Dr. Rosen used Novocaine, and at six-thirty on Saturday my mouth was still twisted into a grotesque shape. I had already bitten a hole in my lip that bled all over my blouse before I noticed. I certainly didn't feel any pain.

I was about to call Tracy for advice on whether or not I should go to the party, when I realized she wouldn't understand a word I was saying. Ever since I got out of the dentist's office no one could understand anything I said. The Novocaine had numbed my mouth to the point where I couldn't control one side of it.

I had to write down what I wanted to say and have Joel relay the messages to Tracy. Then he'd hand me the phone to hear her answers. He charged me a dollar.

First I wrote down: "Ask her if I should go to the party with a twisted mouth."

"Definitely yes," Tracy said. "Scott Wandover called me today and when I told him I was going to Penni's party he said he was, too. So yes, you better go, or I'll cure your problem of numb lips by ripping them off your face." By the way, Scott is Tracy's sort-of boyfriend.

I had Joel tell her that since she put it so nicely, I'd go, and that I'd be ready at seven. Then I had Joel check to make sure her parents were driving both ways, 'cause my parents were going to be out for the evening.

"Yeah, but they said we have to be ready to leave at eleven o'clock," Tracy answered.

I wrote down: "Our parents treat us like babies."

Joel relayed, "Patty said to tell you your parents have to treat you like babies 'cause that's how you act."

"Yeah, I'm sure that's what she wanted you to say, amoeba brain," Tracy yelled into the phone. "Patty," she yelled even louder, to make sure I heard, "you just chill out and everything's going to be fine."

I was so nervous I bet I changed outfits about a dozen times. When Tracy's car pulled into the driveway I was standing over my bed with every outfit I own (not that there were that many) spread out in front of me. I threw on my olive-drab Palmetto top and the matching red-and-olive-plaid pants, shoved on a pair of shoes from the jumble on the floor, and ran out to her car.

In the car I tried not to talk because everything I tried to say was still sounding like my tongue weighed ten pounds.

"It'll be okay by the time we get there," Tracy reassured me.

Her dad had the same reaction as mine when he saw Penni's house: a long, slow whistle. We jumped out of the car and headed for the door, with me saying over and over, under my breath, "I am not nervous. I am not nervous." Only it came out, "I ah nah nuhfuf. I ah nah nuhfuf."

As we waited for the doorbell symphony to end and for someone to let us in Tracy said to me, "I've got a news flash for you.
You *should* be nervous."

"Wah?"

"Look down. You're wearing one red shoe and one black one."

I looked down. She was right. In my hurry I had put on two
different shoes. I wanted the earth to swallow me up right then
and there. I wanted to disappear. I wanted to turn and chase
Tracy's car down the driveway. Instead I unrolled the cuffs of
my pants and tugged down at the waist, trying to force my pants
to cover my shoes.

James opened the door and led us to an enormous wood-
paneled room that had a pinball machine, a real video arcade
game, a Foosball table, a giant-screen television that took up
almost a whole wall, and enough couches and stuffed chairs so
no one had to sit on the floor. At one end of the long room was
a fireplace with a roaring fire.

Penni greeted us. "Come on over here and meet some of my
friends," she said. I tried to shuffle along taking little sliding
steps so my shoes wouldn't show. Then I sat down the first
chance I got and folded my legs under me. I decided not to get
up for the rest of the evening.

"Tracy, I order you to stay next to me all night and get anything I need. I refuse to get laughed at during my first party at
Penni Pendleton's house," I whispered, even though it came out
sounding like I was talking in some kind of tribal language.

I turned to make sure she understood what I had said, but
Tracy had disappeared. I saw her standing with Scott a few feet
away from me.

"Ssst," I hissed. She didn't hear. "*Ssssst,*" I hissed again, a
little louder.

"Are you having a problem?" Penni asked.

"N-no. I ruf juf abbiwing yaw beautipuw hoe."

"What? What on earth are you saying? Why are you making a spectacle of yourself? Patty, this is no time to be silly. Don't you want to impress my friends?"

I tried to say "Novocaine," but it came out "Nowahcayw." I tried to say that I had just been to the dentist, but all I succeeded in doing was getting Penni annoyed. She started to walk away in a huff. I had to get over to Tracy, my interpreter, so I risked showing my feet.

Penni noticed the shoes immediately. She practically shrieked with laughter and said, "Look, everyone, Patty is trying to make a fashion statement. I bet you have another pair just like that at home, don't you? Can I borrow them sometime?" It felt like every one of the fifty or so people in the room was looking at my feet.

I tried to laugh and pretend I thought it was funny. Then I slowly edged my way out of the room. Tracy followed me.

When I got to the foyer I practically started to cry. Tracy put her arm around me. "Don't let Penni ruin the party for you. Just walk back in there like nothing happened. I'll stay right by your side. Not even Scott can drag me away this time. Come on."

I took a deep breath and we went back in. Tracy explained to Penni that I had been to the dentist, and that the shoes were something I read about in a French fashion magazine and it was all the rage in Paris this season. She told Penni she was surprised she hadn't known about it.

Penni left us sitting by ourselves on the couch, which was just fine with me. I figured if I could just sit unnoticed for an hour or so, maybe the Novocaine would wear off and I could accidentally bump into Tim and start up a conversation that would eventually lead to us getting back together again. No such luck. We no sooner sat down than Tracy jabbed me in the ribs and whispered that Tim and Scott were on their way over.

Immediately my scalp started to prickle and my hands got clammy. I could picture big circles of dark sweat forming at the armholes of my shirt.

"Hi," Tim said. "How've you been?"

"We've been fine," Tracy said.

"Do any skiing lately?" he asked, looking at me.

"Not much," Tracy answered.

"It's good to see you," Tim said to me.

"Nice to see you, too," Tracy answered for both of us.

At this point I was ready to kill Tracy with my bare hands. If she didn't explain why I wasn't talking in about five seconds, I was planning on jabbing my fake fingernail into her arm till I drew blood.

"You look great, Patty," Tim said.

"Doesn't she?" Tracy answered. Then, "Oh, I forgot to tell you—Patty's had dental work and can't talk very well." I breathed a sigh of relief. At least Tim would know I wasn't ignoring him.

He stood next to our couch for a couple of minutes, not saying anything, just shifting his weight from one foot to the other, till Penni came over and told him she had a friend she wanted him to meet. I didn't know whether to be relieved or angry that he went with her.

Scott sat with us and talked to Tracy for about the next hour while I stared at the floor, wishing I could be invisible. Every once in a while I'd mumble something to myself, just to see if my speaking ability was coming back, and finally my words started coming out intelligible.

I hoped that Tim would stop back and try talking to me again. But every time I spotted him he was with Penni's friend, Rebecca, who wore matching shoes and hadn't had a cavity filled right before coming to the party.

Penni announced that it was game time, and almost everybody groaned. I wondered why.

"Since Patty and Tracy are new to our little group, they have to do the pretzel game," she called out to everyone. The pretzel game turned out to be a game where you have to eat four pretzels within sixty seconds. It didn't sound like a big deal, and since my Novocaine had worn off, I volunteered to go first.

The first pretzel was easy. I watched the big grandfather clock in the corner and saw that I had swallowed it in fifteen seconds. The second pretzel went a little slower. By the time I stuffed the third pretzel into my mouth forty seconds had gone by and I was getting a little low on saliva. By the fourth pretzel I felt like I was trying to eat a mouthful of cotton. It absolutely would not go down my throat. I started to choke and ended up spraying the crowd with partially chewed pretzel. I was so embarrassed, and everyone was laughing so hard at me, I wanted to die.

Tracy was a good sport and tried the pretzel game after me. She knew better, though, and tried to eat the last pretzel facing away from the knot of people watching. At least when she gagged and blew her lunch it was away from the crowd.

"Okay," announced Penni, "the next game we're going to play is called pinch-your-neighbor's-cheek." We all stood in a circle and had to go around one by one, pinching the cheek of the person to our right. The idea was not to laugh. Every time I pinched Tracy's cheek I had absolutely no desire to laugh. It just wasn't funny. But everyone else was hysterical.

When the game ended Tracy and I flopped onto cushions near the fire. "What was so funny?" Tracy asked me.

"I was just going to ask you the same thing. I laughed just so I wouldn't look out of place."

We were sitting alone, trying to figure out what had been so hysterical, when I saw Scott coming over to us. He sat down next to Tracy and said something in her ear.

Tracy took my face in her hand and turned it so she could see my left cheek.

"Patty, that dork Penni just tried to make a fool of you again. The person next to you had lipstick on her fingers. Every time she pinched your cheek she put a red smudge on it. You look like a clown."

"I'm sorry," Scott added. "I should have said something. Penni thinks it's funny. That's why I hardly ever come to her parties anymore. She likes to invite the football players whether she knows them or not, so Tim and I sometimes get invited. But I don't enjoy coming."

The thought of Tim seeing me get smudged made my whole face turn red. I jumped up and ran out of the room again. Tracy followed me. This time, when I got to the foyer I *was* crying.

"How could she be so mean?" I bawled. "Could you call your father and have him come get us right now?"

Tracy left to search for a phone. I stood by the front door, shaking with humiliation.

"Patty, what's wrong?" It was Penni, standing beside me and touching my shoulder.

"Nothing," I said. "I just have to leave now." I kept my face away from her so she wouldn't have the satisfaction of seeing me cry.

"Patty, I think I hurt your feelings. I didn't mean to. Really didn't. We do this to all the new kids we like. It's our way of initiating them into our group. I thought you'd laugh at it. But apparently you took it in the wrong way. Your shoes, too. I thought you wore them to be funny. I was just going along with the joke." She took both my shoulders and turned me to face her. "I really like you, Patty. I wanted you to be part of the group. Can you forgive me? Please?" She handed me a tissue.

Tracy got back then and right away started railing on Penni.

"Would you just leave her alone?" Tracy said. "You've done enough damage for one night."

"It was a joke," Penni explained.

"Then how come she's not laughing?" Tracy shot back angrily.

I cut in and said, "It's okay, Tracy. She really did mean it as a joke. Let's go back in." Penni led the way. Tracy and I followed, with Tracy staring at me like I was bonkers.

Within a few minutes, though, Tracy's father came and we had to leave. At the door I thanked Penni for a wonderful time and for inviting me and for wanting me to be one of the group. I asked her if I could meet her parents before I left to thank them for the nice party, but she said they were out for the evening.

"You're acting like a wimp," Tracy said as we rode home.

"Am not."

"Are too."

"Am not."

"Are too."

"Am not."

"Someone would think you're her puppet."

"Would not."

"Would too."

"Would not."

"Would too."

"Would not."

"You're wearing blinders, Patty, and don't you dare say 'Am not.' "

I kept my mouth shut and stared out the window the rest of the way home. When Tracy's dad let me out I mumbled "Am not" as I shut the door hard behind me.

I took off my mismatched shoes, washed the last traces of red smudge off my face, brushed the pretzels out of my teeth, and went to bed, wondering if I would ever be cool and classy and fit in with Penni's crowd.

Sunday, the day after the party, I finally won a battle with my mother. I spent all day bugging her to let me get my hair straightened and she finally gave in. It was a struggle, though.

First, she gave me the speech about how great curly hair is, for the kajillionth time. Then she made a confession.

"You think I was put on this earth to stop you from doing all the things you want to do, don't you, Patty?" she asked.

That was exactly what I thought. But I knew better than to tell her so. I kept my mouth shut and just sat at the kitchen table with my knees crossed, swinging one leg and flipping through a magazine like I wasn't listening.

Mom went on, "But the truth is, the reason I don't want you to straighten your hair is that I know from experience how bad it can turn out. When I was your age I straightened my hair one day when my mother wasn't home." I stopped swinging my leg. "I wanted to look like Aunt Carol, who had long, straight hair that swung when she walked and fell over her face and turned boys' heads. I was so jealous." I stopped flipping magazine pages and looked at Mom to make sure she was serious. It was like she was reading my mind. "It turned into a disaster. When I finished straightening my hair and dried it, it didn't swing or fall in my face. It just stuck straight out in spikes and wouldn't take even the slightest curl. I ended up cutting it short."

"That doesn't mean it's going to happen to mine," I said. "You have to let me make some of my own decisions. I'm practically grown up. And if I blow it, it'll be my mistake. I'll take the responsibility."

She finally gave in. "But if it comes out horrible," she warned, "don't come crying to me that you want to quit school and become a hermit in the Sahara Desert for a few months. Remember, it'll be your mistake and you'll have to take responsibility for it."

I ran for the phone to ask Tracy when she could come over and straighten it. Between my baby-sitting job for a faculty member's kids two days a week after school and Tracy's trumpet lessons and ballet class and a paper she had due and a test I had to study for, the first available time was Friday after school. That was fine with me. I'd have all weekend to style my hair and get to know the new me. No one would be seeing me over the weekend except Gary, and he didn't count.

I had told Gary he could come over on Saturday night because Tracy was going to be out of town visiting her brother at college, Kate was going to visit her grandmother in Rochester, and Penni couldn't possibly be having another party so soon. The only condition I put on our working Saturday night was that Gary not go telling people he had a date with me, or even get that thought in his head.

Tracy came home from school with me on Friday. While we were having chocolate milk and Oreos Chris came into the kitchen and made himself a mayonnaise and ketchup sandwich.

"You're making me sick," I told him. "Go eat that thing outside where you won't nauseate people."

"It's a free country," he said, licking the knife clean.

"How do you come up with those clever sayings?"

"I think them up," Chris answered, beaming. My sarcasm went right over his head. He sat down next to Tracy. "Want to know about the contest me and my club are having?" he asked her.

"Not really."

"We're having a burping contest. We're all practicing from now till our meeting next week and then we're gonna give a prize for the longest burp and the loudest burp."

"Thanks for sharing that with me," Tracy said. "What is your club anyway, a culture and manners club?"

"No, we call ourselves The Jokers, because we do fun stuff at our meetings."

"Yeah, I can see that. Burping would be on just about anybody's list of fun things to do," Tracy said.

"Want to hear me burp?"

"Not really."

"Well then, want to come to our next meeting? You could be in the contest, or you could be a judge."

"Uh, no. I'm busy that day."

"I didn't even tell you what day the meeting was."

"Well, I'm busy all next week. Really. It's booked solid. I need an appointment book to keep track of all the things I'm doing next week."

I interrupted, "Look, Chris, what she's trying to tell you is that you're making us sick to our stomachs with this burping stuff, so just vaporize yourself, will you?"

Chris left the kitchen yelling, "Mommm! Patty's calling me names again!"

After our snack Tracy gave me a hair-straightening treatment. We did everything according to the directions, except we left the solution on longer than we were supposed to. I wanted to be sure the stuff had time to do its job. I wanted my hair to be real straight, just like Penni's, so I could sort of swing it around like she does.

When it was done I went upstairs and blew my hair dry. I looked at the result in the bathroom mirror and nearly screamed. My hair looked like it had just been zapped by an electric current. It was straight, but it didn't hang down in a silky mass, the way I had imagined it would. It stuck out in dry spikes, just like my mother had warned me it might. I wet it and blew it dry again. This time I curled it around a styling brush as I dried it. It came out looking like a cheap Cleopatra wig. I went running down the stairs, hysterical.

"Mom, why did you let me do this? Just look at my hair! I look like a freak! Now I have to quit school and wear a paper bag over my head for the next three months!"

Mom and Tracy had looks of horror on their faces, but Mom sat me down and started combing my hair. "It's not so bad," she said calmly. "We'll give it a hot oil treatment and put rollers in it overnight and it'll be fine."

"No it won't. My head looks like cotton candy that got caught in a tornado. It's awful. Tracy, you shouldn't have kept the stuff on so long. I know I told you to, but since when do you listen to me? Oh, I want to die. Mom, promise me you won't make me go to school Monday? Please? Just Monday? Just till I can buy a wig? Please?"

When Tracy left I sat at the kitchen table peeling potatoes for supper and bawling. I barely heard the doorbell ringing or Chris talking to someone. But my ears perked to attention at the sound of Penni Pendleton's voice. She was at the door asking if I was home and Chris was telling her I was in the kitchen. Before I knew it Penni was standing in the kitchen doorway.

She stared at my hair for a long time before she smiled, then snickered, then laughed out loud.

"What have you done to your hair? It looks absolutely pathetic." Without waiting for an answer she shook her head so her silky, shining hair swung gracefully back from her face, and went on. "I'm sorry to drop in without warning, but I wanted to give you this." She handed me an envelope. "It's a poem I wrote. I'd like to submit it to the literary magazine. Patty, it would mean the world to me if it got accepted. My dad says if I get something in *Reflections* he'll buy me a horse. I've been working on this one for weeks." She patted the envelope and smiled at me.

I asked her why she hadn't just put the poem in the submission box at school.

"Well, I wanted you to look it over and make any changes you thought it might need, first."

I told her I couldn't do that. The submissions had to be anonymous. I asked her if she'd put her name and homeroom on a separate page like the rules call for.

She said she had, so I took the envelope from her. Just then my mom came in. "Mom, this is Penni. She's new at school this year."

"Hi, Penni," my mom said. "It's nice to finally meet you. I hope you can stay awhile."

"No, I'll be leaving. I can see you're getting ready for dinner."

"Why don't you stay and eat with us?" Mom asked. "It's no trouble."

In Mom's defense I have to say that she probably had no idea the torment she was causing me. She invited Penni for the simple reason that she has this rule about knowing the friends that Joel and Chris and I hang around with. I think she read it in some book on how to be a good parent. And here was her chance to get to know Penni.

"Patty's just had a disaster trying to straighten her hair and I think she could use some cheering up," Mom went on. Now I wanted the floor to open up and swallow me. I prayed Penni would say no. I hoped she had a riding lesson or a hairdresser appointment, or a meeting with her stockbroker or a flight to the North Pole or something. But no. Penni got this huge smile on her face and went running outside to tell James to leave.

I glared at Mom, but she wasn't paying any attention. She was busy telling me to peel an extra potato and telling Chris to set an extra place. I jumped up and told Chris to use the good china and the cloth napkins. Then I rushed around sweeping the newspapers and mail off the table and kicking a bunch of cookie crumbs under the rug by the sink.

I was dying wondering what Penni would think of the black fingerprints on the refrigerator and the basket of laundry in the hall. I hoped she wouldn't notice that there would be one folding chair at the table. And I seriously asked God not to let Chris tell

Penni about the burping contest, or Mary bug Penni to watch her go on the "big potty."

While I helped Mom get supper ready Mary and Penni played Hungry, Hungry Hippos. Luckily Mary won, so Penni didn't get any marbles thrown at her. Then Mary did the one thing I had prayed she wouldn't. She asked Penni to come and read to her while she went on the big potty.

"Mom, do something," I pleaded. But Mom acted like it was perfectly natural for someone to invite their guest into the bathroom to share an intimate moment.

I could hear Penni upstairs reading from a book of Mother Goose rhymes. Pretty soon I heard Mary tell Penni to clap. I pretty much knew the reason she was ordering Penni to applaud, and I knew that any minute Penni would come running down the stairs saying she had to leave. But instead I heard Penni clap and then laugh. The two of them came back down to the living room. I heard them giggling, and when I went in to call them to supper Penni had Mary on her lap. They were watching a *Leave It to Beaver* rerun. I saw Penni rub her cheek on the top of Mary's head.

"You're pretty," I heard Mary say.

"I am not," Penni answered. "My nose is shaped funny."

Chris looked over from where he was sitting and asked Penni, "Want to hear me burp?" Before she could answer he let out a prize-winning belch. "I'm practicing for a contest," he explained.

"Well, it sounds to me like you have a good chance of winning," Penni answered. She smiled at him. She was acting like a different person from the one she was at school or at her house. I couldn't figure it out.

"I've got an awesome joke," Chris babbled on. "What's the difference between broccoli and nose boogers?"

PROMISES TO KEEP

I quickly called out, "Supper's ready!" before Chris had a chance to give the disgusting answer: Kids don't eat broccoli.

As soon as we all sat down to supper, though, Penni started bragging that she was going to spend eight weeks in Europe next summer and that her father might buy her a horse, and telling us about how her family moves a lot and she's gone to five different schools.

James came to pick her up just as we were eating dessert, and she made him wait in the car for twenty minutes while she finished her chocolate pie. Man, if one of my parents was waiting in the car like that, I'd inhale my dessert.

I walked Penni to the door. "I hope supper was okay," I said. "I hope Mary and Chris weren't too gross. And I want to apologize for the way everybody kept talking at once and interrupting each other. And please forgive Chris for asking if he could touch your hair at the dinner table. He's going through a weenie phase."

Penni didn't answer my apology, just changed the subject and reminded me to turn in her poem.

"I just know it'll get into *Reflections*," she said. "Oh, by the way, I'm having another party in two weeks. You're invited." She opened the door and left.

That night Mom came in as I was looking at my hair in the mirror and trying to smooth it down for about the kajillionth time since I'd straightened it. She sat down on my bed. I groaned, hoping she wasn't there for one of her "talks," where she starts out shooting the breeze and pretty soon is trying to ease me into some kind of deep, meaningful dialogue about my life. I decided I wouldn't do anything to encourage her. I would answer in monosyllables whenever possible.

"Penni was nice," Mom said. "How did you meet her?"

"School," I answered.

"How long have you known her?"

"Awhile."

"She's different from your other friends."

"Mmm."

"Have you met her parents?"

"They're never home."

"I felt a little sorry for her," Mom said, running her hand back and forth across the bedspread.

"You what? That's a laugh. People don't feel sorry for Penni Pendleton, they envy her. She's got everything."

"Don't be so sure of that."

"Like what exactly doesn't she have? I mean, we're talking about people whose car inventory is worth more than our whole house, people who belong to a country club. Her father is some kind of mega executive of a company. When I went to her house I saw three fur coats in the front closet. Penni has looks and loads of friends and she's classy and cool and I would give anything to be in her shoes for a day, just one day."

Mom kept smoothing the bedspread as she explained. "Sometimes kids who move a lot have it rough. They need to prove themselves every time they come to a new school. Sometimes they're insecure. Sometimes, if they have money, it's easier for them to take a shortcut and buy friendship instead of earning it. Penni's lucky to have you for a friend. I think she needs you."

"Mom, you're so totally off base on this. Penni needs me like she needs another ruffly throw pillow on her bed. I'm the one who's lucky. She can have anyone she wants for a friend and she wants me. I think."

Mom didn't say any more. She put on her famous "Mother

knows best" smile, kissed me on the forehead, and left.

Before I got into bed I pulled out my diary and reread my list of resolutions. I put a big star in front of number six—straighten my hair so it sort of swings from side to side like Penni Pendleton's. I checked my hair in the mirror once more, then erased the star.

Looking over the list, I realized I had a long way to go.

12

Most Saturdays I help serve lunch to the poor and homeless at St. Luke's soup kitchen. It started as one of Sister Clarabelle's school projects, but after the project ended I kept going. I got to like some of the guys who ate there, like Charles and Stubs, and I got to be friends with Alex, who's my age and who volunteers there too.

I knew that the guys would have no mercy on me when they saw my hair. I knew they wouldn't be polite and pretend not to notice that I looked like a tribal native from some primitive place untouched by shampoo or conditioner. I was right.

Charles told me my hair looked like his does when he sleeps under the Main Street bridge for a few nights in a row. Har-har.

Alex asked if I got caught under a tree on top of a hill wearing metal shoes during a lightning storm. Har-har.

Even Stubs, who never says anything nasty to anybody, asked

me if I'd like to borrow his hat with the earflaps to hide under. Har-har.

The only person I knew wouldn't make fun was Gary. He thinks I'm so totally gorgeous he wouldn't notice if I was bald.

When Gary came over Saturday night I stuck Penni's envelope in with the pile of submissions we hadn't gotten to yet. As we sat down to work he told me I looked different.

"Do the words 'cotton candy' give you a clue?" I asked.

"It's your hair, I think. Are you wearing your hair a little different?"

"Yeah, you might say that." I changed the subject. "It'll be a little loud here tonight," I explained to Gary as we spread stacks of poems on the table. "Joel and his rock band, and I use the term loosely, are trying to figure out a song to do for St. Iggie's talent show.

"They better hurry. The show's in three weeks."

"It doesn't matter how long they have, they're missing the key qualification for the contest, called talent."

So Gary and I talked about our thoughts for the cover of *Reflections,* and bounced ideas off each other about who the issue should be dedicated to, and read poems while Joel on electric guitar, Dave on keyboard, Dennis ("Boom-boom") on drums, and Rich on sax listened to tapes and tried to decide on a song to slaughter.

Every time they'd stop the tapes and try a few bars of a song, we had no idea what they were playing. Finally Gary yelled down to the basement, "Hey, Joel, you can pick your friends and you can pick your teeth, but you sure can't pick your guitar."

"Watch it, Gar, or you'll be going home tonight wearing Boom-boom's drumsticks up your nostrils," Joel answered.

"Boom-boom plays like he's got them in *his* nostrils," Gary shot back and they both cracked up laughing. A few minutes later Joel yelled up again. "Hey, Gar, come on down and be our vocalist. Maybe you can drown out our lousy playing with your big mouth."

Gary went to the top of the basement stairs and called down over their noise, "Even I'm not that talented."

Gary and I settled into a pattern of reading to ourselves and occasionally reading a poem out loud for the other's opinion. We read to ourselves for a long time till Gary found one he liked.

Sun Cat

In the sunbeam
On the couch
Eyes closed,
to a slit
Ears back
flattened down
Tail switching
aimlessly
Paws curled
under body.
Relaxed.
Ding-dong!
Suddenly
eyes open wide
Ears perk up
tail flies forward
Paws uncurl
Runs to door
Slips outside
Locates sunlight
Lies back down

PROMISES TO KEEP

There was another one we both thought was good, called "The Hole."

Martin Luther King almost filled up the hole.
Many others have tried, all have failed.
The hole that produces hatred and cruelty,
To the ones that are different.

The hole that many children fall into,
Because of the views of their opinionated parents.
The hole that causes jobs to be lost,
And shatters opportunities.

This hole may be filled someday,
Which would bring true meaning to equality.
But, for the bias to change, they must realize,
That they, not us, are the real minority.

When I saw Gary open Penni's envelope and code her poem with a number I pretended to be reading, but I was watching out of the corner of my eye. It didn't matter. I would have known her poem anyway. It was on the same yellow parchment she had used when she wrote me a note about her party.

Gary read the poem and sort of snorted, then slammed it down on the loser pile.

"Bad one, huh?" I asked.

"In a class by itself."

When I reached for it Gary told me not to waste my time, but I read it anyway. Gary was right. If there were a pile on the table worse than losers Penni's poem would go there.

Gary and I dug back into the mountain of submissions and read on. Our eyelids were starting to get droopy when Chris snapped us out of it by sneaking up behind Gary and letting go with a belch that would have registered on the Richter scale.

"Disgusting!" I screeched.

"Awesome!" Gary whooped. "That was world-class. Want to see what I can do world-class?" he asked, standing up. He told us to watch carefully; then he lifted his eyelids by the lashes and rolled his eyeballs upward till they disappeared.

"Yes!" Chris yelled and immediately started trying to make his eyeballs disappear.

"You two are both Neanderthals and I'm leaving before I gag," I said. I went down to the basement and listened to Joel and his friends mutilate every song they attempted. When they tried to play along with "That Old-Time Rock and Roll" Mom and Dad came down and started to dance the way they used to when they were young. It was kind of cute watching them, and pretty soon Gary came down too and we were both tapping our feet and moving our bodies to the rhythm.

"Want to learn some real dancing?" Dad asked us. So we got up and tried their steps. They taught us all the dances that were popular twenty years ago. Gary's a great dancer.

"I'm bushed," Dad finally said. "Play something slower."

Dad took Mom and held her close. They danced like they were alone in the room. It was so beautiful to watch them with their arms around each other and Mom's head on Dad's shoulder. They closed their eyes, and I could almost picture them being young.

Gary took my hand and said, "May I have the pleasure of this dance?" I tried to say no, but he pulled me up from the beanbag chair I was resting in and put his arms around my waist. I put my hands on his shoulders and moved with him to the music.

His shoulders were hard and ripply from lifting weights and he smelled faintly from soap and aftershave lotion. A shiver went through me. I don't know why. It was only Gary.

When the song was almost finished he put his arms tighter around my waist and I moved mine to the back of his neck. My fingers touched the hair at the back of his neck. It was soft. I could feel his breath on my hair. My scalp got all prickly and my hands started to sweat.

When the music ended I dropped my hands down and Gary took his hands from around my waist. He touched my elbows and slowly ran his hands down my arms till his fingers were touching mine. He held them lightly for a few seconds, then let go and jerked his hair out of his face. He walked over to the tape player and started inspecting Joel's tapes.

"That was nice," Mom said to the band. "You boys are getting better."

I stood there looking down at my sneakers and feeling like my whole body was on fire.

"Hey, Gar, sing one with us," Joel coaxed again. "I mean it, you've got a great voice. I've heard you in the summer when your windows are open and you're singing in the shower."

"Nah, I only sound good when I'm naked and wet," Gary said with a laugh.

"No problem. Strip him, guys. I'll go get the garden hose."

"Okay, okay. I'll jam with you. How about something by Billy Joel?"

After about half an hour of Gary singing and the band playing I realized that if any more poems were going to get read I would have to be the one to read them. I slipped away from the rec room and went back to the kitchen table.

Pretty soon Gary came up and we decided to read till we found one more good one. In a few minutes we had, a poem called "While Camping with Friends."

> Tiny white petals
> blow into our hair, into
> our eyes as the trees
> step back to let the wind pass.
> Clouds move in, as thick as clay
> graying the air.
> We run into the cabin.
> The sky lights,
> the trees bend
> and thunder drags across its tracks.
> Rain begins to gather and hum.
> We sit in the window watching and feeling
> safe because we are together.

As Gary put the poem in the "YES!" folder he asked me if I remembered the time when we were about seven and we decided to camp in my backyard one summer night.

"Yeah, I remember. We were going to be so brave that night. We took thermoses of chocolate milk and plastic baggies of Fig Newtons and about ten flashlights out to my little tent and told scary stories till it started to rain."

"Yeah," Gary piped in, "and I told you not to touch any part of the tent or it would start to drip wherever you touched it and you didn't believe me, as usual, so you reached up over your head and touched the canvas and it started to drip on your face, but you wouldn't give me the satisfaction of moving away from the drip. You were stubborn even then."

"Was not."

"Were too."

"And then it started to thunder and lightning and neither of us wanted to be the one to wimp out by saying we were scared," I reminded Gary.

"Boy, was I glad when your father came out and asked us where our common sense was and why we were still out there when we could get fried by lightning at any moment."

"So we went in my house and spread out our sleeping bags on the living room floor and talked about what we wanted to be when we grew up."

"I remember I said I wanted to marry you when I grew up," Gary said.

"Yeah, but I set you straight. I told you I was going to marry my father. Then you laughed and told me I was a doof head, and I got so mad I told you to get out."

"You rolled me right out of my sleeping bag and opened the front door and hurled my sleeping bag out into the storm and pushed me out after it. You had a mean streak even then."

"Did not."

"Did too."

We sat at the kitchen table for a while with our chins resting in the palms of our hands.

"I'm sorry I booted you out into the storm. Forgive me?"

"I'd forgive you anything, Patty."

I looked at him long and hard, straight into his eyes, before I asked, "Would you forgive me if I gave you a criticism, friend to friend?"

"Well, anything but that."

"No, come on, I've been meaning to tell you this for a long time."

"You'll tell me whether I want you to or not, so go ahead."

"It's no big deal, just that your hair would look so much better if you cut that long piece that hangs in your face. Are you aware that you constantly jerk your head to get the hair out of your eyes?"

"I do not."

"Do too. I could trim it for you right now, if you want."

So I got the scissors and draped a towel around Gary's shoulders. I combed his hair, held a long lock of it between my fingers, and snipped.

"Ouch!" he yelped.

"Keep still, or I'll scalp you." I took another snip. I spritzed a little mousse on his hair and combed it back off his forehead. I handed him a mirror.

Gary looked at himself and smiled. "Does this mean you care? Does this mean we're engaged?"

"If I've told you once I've told you a thousand times, I'm marrying my father."

"At least I know enough not to laugh this time. I don't want to end up on my behind out on your front porch."

Gary took the towel from his shoulders and put on his jacket.

"Got to get going," he said as he stacked up the folders of poems. "Can we meet again next Saturday?"

"I guess so, if you don't mind listening to Joel and his friends maim, scar, and mutilate every decent song that's been written in the past five years."

I walked Gary to the front door. "Thanks for the cut," he said as he ran his hand over his new hair style, then reached out and patted mine. "Would you forgive me if I gave you a little criticism, friend to friend?" he asked me.

"No, I wouldn't forgive you."

"Well, I'm going to say it anyway. I think you should curl your hair before you go to church tomorrow."

"I'll think about it," I said as I closed the front door behind him.

13

After three hot oil treatments and three shampoos over the weekend plus three nights of setting my hair on the smallest rollers I could find, it looked passable by Monday morning.

Tracy came over before school to give it a final styling, spraying, and coaxing.

"Do you know how many hot oil treatments I gave my hair over the weekend?" I asked her as we stood at the bathroom mirror.

"Three?"

"I gave it three treatments and it still resembles brown straw. And do you know how much mousse I had to put on it this morning just so it wouldn't stick out all over the place?"

"A whole can?"

"I had to use an entire can. And you know what I'll be forced to do if it won't stay flat, don't you?"

PROMISES TO KEEP

"Transfer to Theodore Roosevelt Junior High, where no one knows you?"

"I'll have to transfer to Theodore Roosevelt Junior High, where no one knows me."

After promising God that I would not gossip for a month if no one at school made fun of my hair, and wrapping a huge scarf tightly around my head, I was ready to head for the bus stop.

"What do you think of Gary?" I asked Tracy as we trudged across the snowy campus.

Tracy looked at me, kind of suspicious. "Why?"

"Never mind. Just drop it."

"I don't believe it," she said, grinning. "You like Gary, don't you?"

"No way. It's just that I've been spending a lot of time with him lately, working on the literary magazine, and he's . . . I don't know . . . different from when we just kid around on the bus and stuff."

Gary came loping up to us just then, so I poked Tracy and made her swear not to say anything to embarrass me.

When we got on the bus Gary tried to squeeze into a seat with Tracy and me, as usual. As usual, I gave him a jab and told him to go find the section of the bus marked "Missing Links."

"What happened to the hair style he's been wearing for the past hundred years? Tracy whispered to me. "His hair looks adorable!"

"I didn't notice," I said, and opened my biology book to study the characteristics of monerans, protists, and fungi.

At lunch no one at my table said a word about my hair. Either it looked normal or Tracy had warned everyone ahead of time to keep their mouths shut.

Penni waved from her table and called me to come over.

"Oh, hi, Penni," I answered real loud, hoping everyone at the tables around us would hear, and would see me sit down next to her and would know that we were friends.

"Did you read my poem?" she asked, beaming. "I really worked hard on it. Is it going to be in *Reflections*?"

I told her I had read it but we hadn't made our final decisions for the magazine yet.

"I know mine will make it." She smiled and winked at me, then reminded me that her next party was a week from Saturday and I could bring Stacy again if I wanted to.

I thanked her and then, just as I was in the middle of telling her that my sister, Mary, had been asking when she was coming over again to play Hungry, Hungry Hippos, Penni's smile turned to a glare and she practically shoved me away, saying that I was blocking someone who was trying to sit down at her table. She turned away from me and started talking to her friends. As I left I heard the word "hair" mentioned and everyone at her table started to giggle.

That week Gary never stopped at my table to bug me, thank goodness. He didn't even walk by, so Penni was spared the job of having to make remarks like, "Where's his Sargeant's flea and tick collar?"

Not much happened that week, other than little events. My hair looked a little better each day, Chris lost the burping contest to his friend Bluto—who won in both the loudest and the longest categories—and I won the bet I had with Joel about Mary and her sweet cereal. On Wednesday at breakfast Mom announced that she would allow Mary to have ten pieces of sweet cereal sprinkled on top of her Cheerios every morning.

"And please," she said to the rest of us, "no speeches about how soft I'm getting and how I never gave in to the rest of you when you were little and how Mary's spoiled. I've already given myself that speech. It's just that I'm getting old and tired and I need some peace. And I did make sure to buy the cereal with the fewest grams of sugar per ounce."

I held out my hand to Joel. "Five dollars, please."

Joel paid me, then picked up Mary's little spoon and asked her, "Now, how does it work, Mary? When you want something all you do is bang this spoon nonstop on a hard surface, screw your face up, and scream till your face turns purple? Okay, I think I've got it."

He poised Mary's spoon in the air and asked Mom if he could have a dirt bike.

I got a letter from Fango and read it to the gang at lunch on Thursday.

Dear Patty,

Thanks for answering my letter. It sounds like you and your friends all want to know how I got started being a bank robber. How come you so intrested? You thinking of a career in banking? Ha-ha.

It all started when I was a kid younger than you. You know how we all want to feel part of a group or just belong? Well I was shy and then this gang of kids wanted to be my friends. Only thing is in order to get into this gang you had to shoplift something. So I go into a K-Mart and take two Milky Way bars. I slide one of them up the sleeve of my jacket and pay for the other one. I walk out of the store real slow then I run like the devil is after me.

That was my first crime. I didnt even eat the candy bar up my sleeve on acount of it melted.

So now Im in the gang. We walk down the street and make fun of other kids who dress funny or look funny or we make fun just cause it feels good to do it. We laff a lot. Packman is our leader and we do whatever he tells us.

We do a lot of shoplifting. We put rubber bands around the cuffs of our pants and rip open the inside of our pants pockets so we can shoplift stuff down our pants leg. We lift clothes and sunglasses and watches so we always wearing the latest stuff and look cool. Dont you go doing that Patty or you got me to answer to. Sometimes we get caught and our mas get called and we got to swear never to do it again, but I want to be in the gang so I do it again. You know how it is, Patty, sometimes all a kid wants is to belong and feel speshal cause other kids notice you and get out of your way.

One time we were walking down the street and we see Alvin. Now I like Alvin. He gets good grades and works at McDonald's and his hobby is figgering out prime numbers, whatever that means I dont know. So we see him walking home in his Mc-Donald costume and we stop him. Packman tells him he got to pay two dollars to walk by us. Alvin says no way. Packman shoves him down and holds a knife on his chest and says think on it a little harder. Alvin looks up at me. He looks so sad I want to run away. But he reaches in his pocket and Packman grabs his wallet and runs off. I still wonder about Alvin. I wonder if he is still figgering out prime numbers. I wish I could tell him Im sorry.

I finelly got sent to Youth Corectional when I was fifteen. One day about six of us go out looking for action. We go into another naborhood and every time we see a kid on a bike we go up to

113

him and start talking. Then we shove him off the bike and one of us takes off on it. If the kid is wearing a watch we take it and I keep all the watches on my arm. We are stupid but we are stoned so we dont know how dumb were acting. We think were hot stuff. A cop came by and didnt think we were such hot stuff especally me with the watches up and down my arm. So I end up at Youth Corectional for a few months.

If your under 18 you cant go to real jail. But as soon as I turned 18 I got arested for beating up a guy to get money for drugs. I got found guilty and put in a drug rehab program. But I could of ended up in jail.

I will tell you how I finelly ended up in jail next time. Right now my fingers are tingly from writing so much so I got to go.

Answer to last trivial question: 2 gallons

New trivial question: What has 336 dimples?

Answer to last riddle: holes

New Riddle: A boy falls off a boat in the middle of a lake. He cannot swim. What is the first thing he does?

from your friend
Fango

PS If your wondering where I get all these riddles and trivial questions I got a book out of the prison libary. I hope your libary doesnt have the same book. Ha-ha.

PS PS Im having a parole hearing. That means I got a chance of geting out of here.

"This gives me the shivers, really, to be hearing how some real person ended up in trouble with the law. It's like peeking into a different world," Jeannie said.

"Yeah," Tracy agreed. "His life is so different from ours."

"I feel sorry for poor Alvin," Whitney said.

"What about poor Fango?" I put in. "I feel sorry for *him*. He was probably such a loser he'd do anything to belong to a gang."

"Yeah, and that Packman probably bullied everybody big-time. I'd like to get my hands on him," Allison said, making fists and jabbing at the air.

"I'm dying to know about him and dope. Ask him to tell about that in his next letter, Patty," Trish instructed me. "And be sure to ask how much money he got from robbing banks and if it's still hidden someplace. I saw a movie once where this guy wouldn't confess where he hid the money and the only thing that kept him going in prison was knowing that he'd be rich when he got out. After ten years he got out and went to where he and his girlfriend had hidden the money, only she had taken it and run off with his best friend."

Tracy hit Trish with her paper bag.

"I can't wait for his next letter," said Kate as we left the cafeteria. "This is getting almost as good as *Days of Our Lives*."

When I got home from school I answered Fango's letter. I told him about all my friends, including Penni and Tim. I told him my New Year's resolutions. I told him I hoped he didn't mind me writing so often, but my friends and I looked forward to his letters.

During that week I worked on getting my parents to become more refined and genteel, and a little classier, just in case Penni ever visited us again. I talked to Dad about what a dead-end job he was in and how he should spread his wings and experience life, for Pete's sake, by becoming a bank executive or a company president.

Dad said he'd never thought about it before but would give it careful consideration. Then he went back to fixing a broken lamp plug.

I also dragged Mom's winter coat out one night after dishes and told her it was an embarrassment. The darned thing was five years old, I told her, and besides, wasn't she at that stage in life where she deserved something more, something like a leather coat, for instance? I told her about a sale I had seen at the mall and even offered to go with her to pick one out. Mom was folding laundry on the kitchen table, and without looking up she told me she'd give it careful consideration.

"And while we're on the subject," I added, "have you ever thought about taking your proper place in this community by joining a country club?"

"Just what subject are we on, anyway?" Mom wanted to know.

"The subject of people's station in life, people's position in the community, people's social consciousness," I explained patiently. "I mean, don't you and Dad have any ambitions? Don't you want to move up the ladder of success?"

"Don't we want to try harder to impress others? No. Now start trying to impress your mother by folding these towels and putting them in the linen closet."

I folded them, mumbling to myself that the least we could do was buy monogrammed linens.

During that week Gary came over on Tuesday night and on Wednesday after school to work on *Reflections*. He showed me a beautiful photo he had found of a lake with trees reflected on the surface of the water. We decided to use it on the cover. He also told me Mrs. Nielsen had picked a layout editor.

While he was at my house he helped Dad fix a leak under the

powder room sink and coached Chris for his next competition—long-distance spitting. He taught Mary a dumb knock-knock joke that she repeated every five minutes for the next two days. And he taught me a judo move to use in case I was attacked from behind.

On Friday night Gary called to make sure we could get together on Saturday to work. I said I was expecting him. That night, as I was falling asleep, the last thing that drifted through my head was a picture of Gary putting his arm around me to demonstrate the judo move.

14

When Gary came over on Saturday night he handed me an envelope and told me it was his submission to the magazine and I was to read it after he left. He wanted me to give my absolute honest opinion of it and I promised I would.

I set out a plate of Oreos and two glasses of milk and we started reading poems. At this point our stack of rejects was a mile high, the pile of possibles had a couple dozen poems, and the "YES!" category had fewer than ten.

We worked for two hours without adding a single poem to the "YES!" pile. Finally Gary got up, rubbed his eyes, and suggested we take a break and go downstairs to mock out Joel and his friends. He took his earmuffs out of his jacket pocket, put them on, and headed for the rec room. I could hear Boom-boom's voice greet him with, "Very funny." Joel told Gary he couldn't wait till the talent show so he could stuff their first-prize trophy down his throat and jam the earmuffs in after it.

I put our milk glasses in the dishwasher, combed my hair and put on some lipstick, then went down to the rec room. Gary was singing while the group tried unsuccessfully to back him up.

"The Rolling Stones you're not," I informed them. "And you're no Mick Jagger," I said to Gary.

"Hey, let's do one together," he suggested, and pulled me over to the microphone hooked up to the sound system.

I refused, but Gary went over to the pile of tapes on the counter and put one in the tape deck. He fast-forwarded it till he found the song he was looking for. Then he put his arm around my shoulder and started singing "The Next Time I Fall." I absolutely love that song.

I pulled the microphone closer to me and joined in.

"Hey, you guys aren't bad," Rich said. "Let's try it together."

Gary and I sang it again while Joel's group tried to play backup.

"This could work," Joel decided. "All along it was Patty's big mouth that we needed to drown out our lousy playing. Let's do it one more time."

By now Gary and I were really getting into it. We put some moves into the act and tried to do them in time with each other. We flung our arms out and swayed together to the music. When it was over we collapsed laughing.

"Is there an agent in the house?" Gary called out.

Joel and his friends started begging us to be in the talent show with them. They were serious. I was serious too, when I said, "No way."

PROMISES TO KEEP

I went upstairs and started straightening out the piles of poems. Gary came in and sat down at the table.

"What do you say we do it?" he asked. "It would be fun. We could put together a real routine."

"I don't think so, Gary. Really."

"Okay, we could do a different song. We could do 'That's What Friends Are For.'"

"Really, I can't."

"Why not?"

"Don't ask. Just take my word for it. I can't do it." I sat there biting my nails and pretending to read a poem while Gary stared at me.

"And will you quit staring at me?" I said sharply.

"Sorry," Gary said. "And I'm sorry I asked. I think I understand why you can't do it."

"You don't understand anything, Gary Holmes."

"Yes I do. I understand completely. I've heard Penni's remarks when I walk by her in the cafeteria. You don't want to be seen on the stage with me. It might hurt your image with your new friend. You care so much about what she thinks you can't even think for yourself anymore. Your problem is, you don't know who your friends are. You don't know who really cares about you."

Gary got up, put on his jacket, and walked out of the kitchen. He came back and jammed on his earmuffs in front of me before storming out again. I jumped as the front door slammed behind him.

I sat at the table shaking. I tried reciting the Gettysburg Address to keep from crying, but it didn't work. Tears formed at the corners of my eyes and plopped down on the table in front of me. They plopped down on Gary's envelope. I wiped the back of my hand across my face and opened it. I read Gary's poem.

> There must be someplace
> Where our souls can rest
>
> At this place tears
> don't fall and
> pain don't rise
>
> an' love won't never go
> unanswered

"Why are you doing this to me, Gary? It's not fair," I said, crumpling up the paper. "It's not fair. I can be friends with whoever I want, and I can *not* be friends with whoever I want, and my reasons are nobody's business, especially yours, Gary Holmes."

I sat at the table rearranging the three Oreos left on the plate and giving Gary a piece of my mind. "Did you ever stop to think what kind of person I want you to be? Did you ever try to be that kind of person? No. So just don't expect me to fall all over you."

I wished Gary had never asked me to be coeditor with him. I wished he had never shown me the judo move or danced in the rec room with me. I wished he had never put his arm around me and sung "The Next Time I Fall." I wished I had never felt his warm breath in my hair. I wished Gary would just leave me alone.

"Hey, where's Gary?" It was Joel, wanting Gary to come down and sing with them.

"He left a few minutes ago."

"Oh, I heard you talking. I didn't realize you were just having a conversation with a plate of Oreos. Sorry."

I got up and went to my room. I unwadded Gary's paper and

smoothed out the wrinkles. I copied the poem on a sheet of filler paper to submit to the magazine, and put the original in my drawer of small important things. It smelled faintly of aftershave lotion.

15

On Sunday Kate, Tracy, Trish, and I went to a movie. Afterward we all squished into a booth at Ben's Burgers to pig out on Ben's Super Sizzleburgers and talk about—what else?—boys.

Here's the situation for each of us: Tracy has Scott who is sort of interested in her and she's sort of interested in him, but they don't make a big deal of it.

Kate wishes this guy named Kevin, who her father hired to shovel their driveway, would notice her. Kevin is supposed to shovel every morning after it snows so Mr. Donnelly can get out of the driveway to go to work. So Kate gets up every morning at five-thirty to see if it snowed during the night. If it did she goes outside and starts shoveling, just to get Kevin to notice her. When Kevin comes he sits around and watches her do the work; then he gets paid. We've told Kate how ridiculous she is, but she just doesn't see it.

PROMISES TO KEEP

Trish talks a lot about boys, but we all think that if a guy ever walked up to her and said hi she'd run away from fright.

As for me, well, you know my situation. Tim dumped me for the ski slopes, but every time I see him my knees still turn to Jell-O. Alex, the volunteer at the soup kitchen, is a super guy, but he's just a friend.

Then there's Gary, who I don't even want to talk about. He is just the most unreasonable person I have ever met. I mean, asking me to sing with him at the talent show was the last straw. Yes, he's fun and yes, he's interesting and yes, he has great muscles and yes, he has exactly the same sense of humor as me, but that's it.

I wouldn't want to be seen on the stage with him and have people think I like him or anything like that. He's just not the sort of guy I'd fall for. And it isn't only because he's my neighbor and we've grown up together and we've made fun of each other all our lives and when we were three we once took a bath together and my mother took a picture of it, which she hid because if I ever find it I will tear it into a kajillion pieces. And it isn't because Penni called him a nerd and I'm trying to be like Penni.

It's the earmuffs and the short-sleeved shirts in winter and the way he jerks his hair out of his eyes every ten seconds— well, used to, until I cut his hair. And lots of other things which I can't think of this very minute. But Penni Pendleton has absolutely nothing to do with it.

At Ben's, while everyone talked about who their ideal date would be for the spring dance in March, I just sat there dragging a french fry back and forth through a puddle of ketchup. When Kate mentioned Gary's name I got up and went to the ladies' room.

On Monday when I walked into the school cafeteria I couldn't believe my eyes. Gary was sitting with Kari Kunde. They were alone at a table and had their heads bent toward each other as they talked. I decided that if Gary was doing it for my benefit I wasn't going to give him the satisfaction of even looking that way. I flipped through my books all the while I walked to my table, pretending I was looking for something. I only bumped into one person and I'm sorry the person had a full lunch tray in her hands and I made her spill her soup, but at least I made it to my table without looking anywhere near Gary.

As soon as I sat down Penni motioned for me to come to her table. She waved a girl off the chair next to her and patted it for me to sit down. I looked over at Tracy and her eyes were bugging right out of her head. I think she was thinking I was going to start sitting at Penni's table for lunch, which I would never do.

"How was your weekend?" Penni asked.

"Fine," I said.

"Did you work on *Reflections*?"

"Yeah."

"Well, did you make a decision on my poem?"

My hands suddenly got sweaty and I wondered why I was petrified to tell Penni we had rejected her poem.

"Well, it's this way, Penni," I said, so quietly that she asked me to speak louder. "It's this way. There were about a kajillion entries and yours was very interesting, but we had an awful lot of poems about the beauty of new-fallen snow and yours just missed getting chosen."

At first she asked me, very nicely, if there had been some kind of mistake. When I told her there hadn't, and that I shouldn't even be telling her the results but I was doing it because we were such good friends, she asked me if I could help her change it and make it better, then resubmit it.

"You're so talented, Patty. Really. I envy you. I know you could add just the right feeling to my poem. You could bring out what I tried to picture. Help me just a little itty bit, please?"

"I really don't think I could," I said. "Maybe next year you can try again."

Penni pulled her chair closer to mine and put her hand on my arm as she said, "Hey, I just got a great idea. Remember how great we worked together on my report? Well, maybe you could come over some night and we could throw some ideas back and forth and, instead of a poem, I could write an essay for *Reflections*. We're totally on the same wavelength and we had so many of the same ideas for the report. I know we could come up with something great. Hey, what sign are you? I bet we're even the same sign."

"I'm Gemini."

"I knew it. So am I. We are so tuned in to each other! I know you could get my writing juices flowing. I just need your spark to get started. What do you say? Afterward we could go for a swim in my indoor pool. Can you come tomorrow night?"

"Penni, the deadline for submissions is past," I explained.

"Oh, come on. You're not going to let a little thing like that bother you. You're on the staff. No one would know. It's no big deal."

"I'm sorry, Penni. You're going to have to wait till next year."

Penni's face turned red and her mouth twisted up real weird. She spoke to me through clenched teeth, so she hissed as she talked. "Next year? I am going to have my poem in this year. My father wants me to get something in this year and I will. I'll go over your head. Who's in charge of the magazine?"

"Gary Holmes."

Penni burst out laughing. "I should have known. Well, we'll just see what Gary Holmes decides." She waved me out of the chair and added, "And by the way, the party's been canceled."

Penni went to Gary's table and bent down close to his face so her hair brushed against his arm as she talked. I couldn't hear what she said and I couldn't hear Gary's answer. All I saw was Penni flip her hair over her shoulder and glide down the aisle with everyone's eyes on her.

I felt sad the rest of the day, so sad I could barely drag myself from class to class.

When I got home I went to Joel's room and knocked on his door.

"Yeah?" he answered.

"Can I come in?"

"Who is it?"

"It's Patty, you idiot. Who does it sound like?"

"Yeah."

"Yeah, what?"

"Yeah, you can come in. That's what you asked, isn't it?"

Joel was sitting at his desk counting his paper route money. I sat down on his bed.

"How much do you need this time?" he asked without looking up.

"I don't need a loan. I just want to talk." Joel stopped counting his money and leaned his chair back on two legs.

"Joel, am I popular?"

"Aw, jeez, Patty, I hate when you try to get me into these weird discussions. Why don't you write to Ann Landers?"

"Okay, let me ask you an easier one. How far would you go to keep a friend?"

"Oh, that's much easier, thank you. Come on, get down to specifics."

"Okay, let's say you want something really badly, but to get it you have to sort of break a rule."

"You're not making this easy, Patty. I have no idea what you're getting at."

"Okay, let me put it more clearly. If you wanted to stay friends with someone, would you do something for her that was against your better judgment, because the thing was very important to the friend?"

"Wait a minute. Does this have to do with some scheme you and Tracy have cooked up? If it does don't tell me another word, or I'll be an accessory to the crime."

"No, it has to do with Penni Pendleton. She wants me to do something that's a teeny bit wrong."

"I'm the wrong person to ask because from what little I know about her from school, I think Penni's a doink. I think she uses people."

"But maybe I think it's okay for her to use me. Maybe I'm getting something out of it."

"That's up to you to decide. Nobody can do it for you. Hey, speaking of deciding, have you changed your mind about singing with Gary?"

"Don't ask, okay? One problem at a time is enough." I sighed and got off his bed. He threw me a quarter as I left the room. "Here," he said. "When I can't make a decision I flip a coin."

"Patty, phone," Mom called up the stairs. "It's Penni."

I took the phone into the closet and bit my nails for a few seconds before answering.

"Mad at me?" Penni asked with a tinkly laugh.

"No, not really."

128

"That's good, because I was hoping you'd think over what I said. Getting into *Reflections* is really important to me, and Gary said it was okay with him to turn in a late submission if it was okay with you. What do you say?"

"Well . . ."

"It's very important to me. It means my dad will buy me a horse of my very own just for having a poem in a crummy school magazine. If you were really my friend you'd do it. You're just trying to act high-and-mighty, aren't you? Just because you're the editor you think you're hot stuff."

I didn't answer.

"Don't you?" she shrieked in a shrill voice. "You're jealous of me, so you're finding a way to act like you're important. Well . . ." She stopped talking; then her voice softened and she said, "Just think about it, okay? I'd let you ride my horse whenever you want. Hey, would you like to come over tonight and swim in my indoor pool?"

"I can't."

"We'll talk again tomorrow. Just think about what I asked. And think about the party on Saturday. I was just kidding about it being canceled. I'll introduce you to the whole football team. I have a feeling one of them is interested in you. 'Bye, Patty."

I went into the kitchen and sat at the table with a glass of milk and a brownie, trying to figure out what to do.

"Is something wrong?" Mom asked.

"No, why?"

Mom pointed to the table, where I had just crumbled my brownie into a kajillion little pieces.

"It's just Penni," I said, not wanting to give away too much information to Mom. "One minute she's nice and the next minute she's nasty. And she always wants things her own way."

PROMISES TO KEEP

"Patty, you know how Mary has a tantrum or throws the marbles when she doesn't win at Hungry, Hungry Hippos? We all act like that when we're three, but as we grow up most of us change. We realize that we're not the center of the world. We learn to give and take and compromise. Maybe Penni hasn't had to learn that yet. It's not right, but it's not totally her fault."

"Yeah, but that doesn't make it any easier to be her friend."

I got up and brushed the brownie crumbs into my hand. I dumped them in the trash and went into the living room. Mary was playing house with her stuffed animals. She asked me to play, but only if she could be the mommy and I the kid, and when I said I didn't feel like it she stomped her feet and let out a scream that I bet Gary could hear four doors away.

I went to my room to be depressed in peace and quiet.

16

The next day I steered the gang to a lunch table in the farthest corner of the cafeteria, to avoid seeing Penni. Gary didn't even show up at lunch. I think he was avoiding me.

When I got home from school there was a letter from Fango on the hall table. I took it up to my room and read:

Dear Patty and friends,

It looks like I got a fan club over there at St. Iggie. Ha-ha.

I told you I would tell you how I got into robbing banks so here goes. I got into big trouble because of dope.

I started drinking beer when I was twelve years old. Beer is a drug—dont let anybody tell you diffrent. You can be a beer addict same as a heroin addict. My gang use to meet after school and pool our money and find sombody legal to buy us a couple six packs. Beer makes us laff and everything seems real funny and you got no problems in the world for a few hours.

Pretty soon we graduate to wine. We always put all our money together to buy stuff and it seems okay cause your doing it with your buddies and not alone.

After awhile we try smoking reefer. By the time Im 18 Im on coke and then heroin.

At 18 I got arested for beating up a guy to get money for dope. Im guilty but insted of jail I get put in a detox program. After that I swear to go clean. I move away from the naborhood. I get a job. I take an art course. Im okay for a couple years. Then one day I meet up with Packman. He says come on down to so-and-sos house. I think Im strong now. So I go, cause Im lonely and I miss the fun of the gang.

So guess what—Im not so strong after all and pretty soon Im an addict again. A gang can have a lot of power over one person.

One day Packman says lets rob a bank and Im high so it sounds like a pretty good idea. The next day it dont sound so good but Im afraid not to go along with what Packman says, plus I need money for dope.

Three of us rob the bank. One of us is in the car. One of us is look out. And one of us does the dirty work. I get picked to do the dirty work.

Im so scared I practicly go to the bathroom in my pants. I hand the teller a note and she gives me a bunch of money.

We rob banks for two years before I get caught. But I remember the looks on every one of them bank tellers faces and I wish to God I could go back and tell every one of them Im sorry. Those women think they might die. They probly go home and have nightmares.

132

Pretty soon I see my face on wanted posters. I cant go out during the day no more.

One day a friend calls me up to meet him. I go out and I think Im being followed. I go into a building. A guy follows me. My hands are starting to sweat and everything starts spining around cause I know its all over. Hes a detective and he grabs me right in front of a bunch of people by the elevater. I think my friend set me up.

For awhile Im in a dream world. I pretend there going to let me go. I picture them coming into my jail cell and telling me its a mistake. I picture a helicopter coming down and reskuing me. But that dont happen. I get a trial and get found guilty. This time I get Smithville and here I am.

Patty, that is my story. I hope you can use it some day when your a famus writer.

You wrote me your new year resolutions and they sound like you got a big job on your hands for the next 12 months. Sounds like your trying to do a snow job on some chic Penni and be in with her group. This is okay so long as she isnt no Packman. I know your smarter then me and I know you come from a diffrent famly and your life is like black and white from mine. But listen, only person you got to impress is yourself cause thats the person you got to look in the eyeball every morning in the miror. All the time I spent being Packmans shadow and now Im inside and hes outside and he dont send me so much as a picture postcard.

Promise me you wont never be stupid like me. Come on, hand on your heart, no fair crossing your fingers—Okay so enough preaching. Im sounding like Saint Fango. I never liked it when my ma or anybody preach to me. I let it go in one ear and come floating out the other. You probly do that too.

PROMISES TO KEEP

I had my parole hearing so I might be geting out of here. If I do maybe I wont be writing to you no more so I wont put a new riddle or nothing in this letter. You know why I always put a riddle and a trivial question? I did it so youd write back just to find out the answer. I like geting your letters. I keep them under my matress and read them every night.

In case this letter is goodby and you dont hear from me no more I want to tell you that you were the only friend I had in the last four years. Well no sense getting all slobbered up over it.

I dont tell this to no one else but you—Im scared to get out of here. This is hell but whats outside is scary too. Could you pray to that St. Iggie person or whoever you pray to and ask him would he sort of keep an eye on me?

Answer to last riddle: Gets wet

Answer to last trivial question: a golf ball

> *Your friend*
> *Fango*

I read the letter through twice. Then I lay down on my bed and stared at the ceiling for a long time, thinking. I thought about Packman and Penni, and about Fango and me. I thought about how when you come right down to it, everybody's problems are sort of the same. I walked slowly downstairs and took the phone into the closet. When I dialed Penni's number she answered on the first ring.

"Hi, Penni," I said. "This is Patty. I'm calling to—"

"Look, will you help me or won't you? I think you've kept me dangling long enough," she interrupted.

I took a deep breath. "It wouldn't be fair to the others who worked to get their submissions in on time. No, Penni, I can't help you and I can't turn in anything you write now that the deadline's past."

Penni exploded. "Well, you can forget about ever swimming in my pool. You and that mongrel friend of yours, Gary, are two of a kind. You deserve each other. You deserve being editors of that stupid magazine too. I don't even want anything of mine in that dumb *Reflections*. And you can tell Gary for me that he's not invited to my party after all. If he showed up it would make me sick to my stomach for the whole night. The two of you are nothing but . . . but . . . zits on the face of life."

As soon as Penni finished her tirade she slammed down the receiver.

"Good-bye, Princess Penni," I said into the dead phone.

I grabbed my jacket and ran over to Gary's house. I told him about the phone call.

"Penni told me you'd take her late submission if I would agree to it. Did you say that?" I asked, even though I was pretty sure of the answer.

Gary shook his head. "I told her I wouldn't and then she said that you said it was okay."

"I hate to break this to you," I said, "but you and I have been officially declared zits on the face of life."

"Well, at least we stand out."

"Furthermore, and I hope you won't break down and cry when I tell you this, you've been uninvited to Penni's next party."

"Oh darn," Gary answered. "And I spent all day trying to think of the perfect birthday present to bring."

"It was a birthday party?" I squawked. "Penni told me she was a Gemini, like me. And my birthday's not till June."

Gary and I stood in his front hall, he with his hand on the doorknob, jiggling it back and forth, and me standing close to him, braiding the fringe on my scarf. For a minute neither of us said anything more; then Gary told me he was sorry for getting mad at me the other day.

"No problem. Hey, that's what friends are for."

Gary and I looked at each other, smiled, and started to sing "That's What Friends Are For" together. We put our arms around each other's waists and went into a routine like we had in my basement. Gary's mom came out of the kitchen, looked at us like we were bonkers, and went back, shaking her head.

After we finished the last bar we stood there with our arms still around each other's waists. Gary didn't move and I didn't move. I looked up at him and asked if it was too late to change my mind about being in the talent show.

"Well, we can sing together but on certain conditions," he said. "We do not tell anyone at school we're doing it, we do not talk about it at school, we do not practice where anyone will see us together, and you are not to touch me—and that one is for your own good."

My face turned red. Gary was telling me the things I had told him when I agreed to work on the literary magazine with him. I pulled my arm away from his waist. He put it back and told me I was losing my sense of humor.

"I can't help it. I lose all my senses when I'm with someone who smells like he fell into a whole vat of cheap aftershave lotion."

"Oh yeah? Well, I lose my cookies when I'm near a girl who's got a three-inch hair growing out of her nose."

"You're perverted."

"You're cute."

Gary gave me a bear hug. We agreed to meet at my house

that night to practice for the talent show and to start looking at the essay submissions for the literary magazine.

"And Gary," I said before I closed the door behind me, "do you forgive me for being such a dweeb? I mean about us, and Penni, and the earmuffs, and, well, everything?"

"There's nothing to forgive. And I'll let you in on a secret about the earmuffs. They were a Christmas gift from my grandparents, and my big brother Sam bet me I wouldn't have the guts to wear them to school for a week without telling anyone it was a bet."

"Did you win?"

"No, you made me lose ten bucks."

"It was the best ten bucks you ever lost, believe me. I mean, don't you care what people think of you?"

"It depends on the people. I care a lot what you think of me."

"I guess for a while there I cared a lot what Penni Pendleton thought of me, and look where it got me. I realize now that Penni is nothing but a sleazoid and I'm an idiot."

"You got that wrong," Gary corrected, smiling. "You're a zit on the face of the earth, remember?"

"Okay, let's get this down straight once and for all. Penni is a sleazoid, I'm a zit, and you're a pathetic zit who makes people sick to their stomachs. Do I have it right?"

"Vividly."

"Did I tell you what my mom thinks about Penni? She feels sorry for her. Can you believe it? She thinks—now get this— she thinks Penni needs me, because of moving all the time and her parents traveling so much. She thinks Penni doesn't know how to relate to people except by bribing them to be her friends. Man, my mother thinks she's a regular Ann Landers."

Gary didn't answer right away. He seemed to be considering what I had said.

"It's something to think about," he finally answered.

"You're kidding. Forget it. Don't go putting ideas into my head. There's nothing to think about. Penni is a sleazoid. She treated us like scum. There's no way I'm going to make excuses for her. . . . Well, I better go. Clarabelle's having us make valentines for a nursing home. I've got to get started cutting hearts out of construction paper."

We both stood there for a few seconds, not saying anything. I pulled up my knee socks. Gary jerked his head back, even though there was no hair in his eyes anymore. Finally he turned the doorknob he'd been jiggling and opened the front door. A blast of cold air made me shiver. Gary reached out and tucked my scarf into my jacket before he closed the door behind me.

When I got home the first thing I did was pull out my list of resolutions. I ripped it up into a kajillion pieces and flung them out the window. A gust of wind caught them and carried them away.

"Toodles," I called out to them as I shut the window.

After supper Gary came over to rehearse our song for the talent show and to work on the essay submissions for *Reflections*. I was just taking my World's Greatest Classics off the shelf and packing them into boxes when I heard him come in the front door and yell, "Yo, Dillmans! Hi to any of you who can hear me!" I heard five voices call back greetings. I ran downstairs to meet him. I had some promises to keep.

At St. Iggie's annual talent show to raise money for kids with muscular dystrophy Gary and I and Joel's band made turkeys of ourselves doing "That's What Friends Are For" in front of a full house.

Tracy and Scott were in the audience. So were Tim and his new girlfriend, Rebecca. Penni was there too. I had asked her to come, and to come to a victory party at my house afterward.

My mom had suggested I invite her and I'd thought about it for a long time before making the call. I tried to put myself in her shoes and imagine how it must feel to move every couple of years and have my parents away all the time and live in a big house with just butlers and cooks and maids to talk to, and be instantly labeled "rich kid" wherever I went. I thought about what Fango said about being friends for the right reasons. I thought about what Mom said about Penni being just as insecure as the next person.

In the end I decided I would try to make a friendship where we were both equal and she could count on me to be honest with her. I had been totally hyper about making the call, though.

"Why are you acting so nice to me all of a sudden, when you wouldn't even put my poem in your magazine?" she'd asked defensively when she answered the phone.

"I just thought you might want to come to my party, that's all."

"I'm mad at you," she said.

"Well, if you get unmad before the talent show, will you come?" I asked.

"What do you want from me?"

"Nothing."

"Is this some kind of trick?"

"No trick. Nothing up my sleeve."

"But I called you names."

"So does my brother and he's invited."

"I'll think about it," Penni said.

The next day she had called to say she'd come.

We didn't win the talent show. First prize went to some girl who played a movement from a Bach concerto for violin. My guess is she bribed the judges. Second prize was won by a couple of seventh graders acting out a scene from *A Christmas Carol*, by my buddy Charles Dickens. It was awesome and I decided maybe C.D. isn't so bad after all.

Even though we didn't win, we had an awesome time. As we stood in the wings after our performance, Gary with his arm around my shoulder and me with mine around his waist, we listened to the applause and grinned at each other. I felt so happy I thought I'd explode.

Gary bent down and kissed me on the top of my head. This time I didn't stomp on his foot.